Tomorrow YOU DIE

You Are a Traitor... and Traitors Are Shot

REONA PETERSON JOLY

YWAM Publishing is the publishing ministry of Youth With A Mission. Youth With A Mission (YWAM) is an international missionary organization of Christians from many denominations dedicated to presenting Jesus Christ to this generation. To this end, YWAM has focused its efforts in three main areas: 1) Training and equipping believers for their part in fulfilling the Great Commission (Matthew 28:19). 2) Personal evangelism. 3) Mercy ministry (medical and relief work).
For a free catalog of books and materials write or call:
YWAM Publishing
P.O. Box 55787, Seattle, WA 98155
(425) 771-1153 or (800) 922-2143
e-mail address: 75701.2772 @ compuserve.com

Tomorrow You Die

Published by YWAM Publishing
P.O. Box 55787, Seattle, WA 98155, USA

ISBN 0-927545-92-6

Printed in the United States of America.

Contents

Foreword

It took Goliath to reveal the commitment of David to his God.

When two young women, a schoolteacher and a nurse, heard the arrogant atheistic roar of a few tyrannical leaders of Albania, their fear of God would not let the boast go unchallenged. Armed with prayer and the "smooth stone" of God's Word, they challenged the "giants in the land."

I first met Reona Peterson Joly at a YWAM outreach in her hometown of Auckland, New Zealand, in 1967. I watched her commitment to Christ as she left the security of her homeland, first to witness to drug addicts on the streets of New York City with Teen Challenge and later to work with YWAM teams in the West Indies sharing Christ. Reona blessed my life and ministry as she conquered the monumental challenge of correspondence from my office as my personal secretary. It was then that I learned to appreciate her depth of relationship with Jesus and her Christlike character on a day-by-day basis.

Reona visited communist nations for the first time while on an outreach trip after attending a training school in Switzerland. It was in prayer that God began speaking to Reona of the hurts, wounds, and bondage of the people of Albania. Trapped by the 1944 takeover of the Albanian government by a clique of dictatorial revolutionaries, the Albanians were told they could never worship God again. The threat of death to those who disobeyed was not an idle boast.

Tomorrow You Die is a vivid testimony to the great love God has for the people of Albania. While darkness engulfed this precious people, God sent two young women behind man-erected barriers as small shafts of light.

To call Reona and Evey extraordinary would be to miss reality. This is the story of two ordinary women on a dangerous mission in obedience and faith to an extraordinary God.

David the giant killer said in Psalm 99:1—

"The Lord reigns, let the people tremble" (NASV).

Loren Cunningham
Founder, Youth With A Mission
Lausanne, Switzerland

Thus says the LORD to Cyrus His anointed,
Whom I have taken by the right hand,
To subdue nations before him,
And to loose the loins of kings;
To open doors before him so that gates will not be shut:
"I will go before you and make the rough places smooth;
I will shatter the doors of bronze, and cut through their iron bars.
And I will give you the treasures of darkness,
And hidden wealth of secret places,
In order that you may know that it is I,
The LORD, the God of Israel, who calls you by your name."

"I am the LORD, and there is no other;
Besides Me there is no God.
I will gird you, though you have not known Me;
That men may know from the rising to the setting of the sun
That there is no one besides Me.
I am the LORD, and there is no other."

—Isaiah 45:1-3,5-6 (NASB)

CHAPTER ONE

I Have Placed Before You an Open Door

It was the jolting of the bus over a particularly large pothole that awakened me.

For several hours the sun had mercilessly streamed in through the bus window as we traveled south from Dubrovnik down the Adriatic coast. There was nothing to break the monotony of the landscape. Marshlands stretched in both directions as far as the eye could see. Scrubby vegetation struggled for life in gray, oozy mud right up to the edge of the narrow road. An occasional seabird broke the silence with its mournful cry. Surely we must be in no-man's-land—a narrow ten-kilometer corridor that separates southern Yugoslavia from Albania.

With little effort, my companion and I were both wide awake. Through our minds in rapid succession flashed the challenges and considerations, the discussions and decisions that had brought us to this moment in our lives. Our hands had been put to the plow, and there could be no turning back.

Without warning, the bus stopped. Through the bus window, we could see a cluster of white cement buildings flanked by rolling gray-blue hills. A large red flag with its imprint of a black double-headed eagle and a single star outlined in yellow fluttered from a tall flagpole. Within seconds the bus was surrounded by soldiers, guns at their sides.

We left the bus carrying our own luggage and were required to walk in front of more soldiers. It was some time before we realized that our clothing was being scrutinized to determine whether the style was "bourgeois." Many passengers were required to reenter the bus and change into something less Western. Color and cut were of particular concern; frowned upon were bright, gaudy colors and smartly styled clothing—especially flared trousers, on either men or women. A few unfortunates had nothing in their suitcases acceptable to the guards, and they were ordered to buy Chinese-made jeans which were on sale at the border to meet the emergency.

Then a barber appeared and was assigned the task of making sure all the men were beardless and had hairstyles above the ears. A strong protest came from one of the group. He had inquired at the Albanian Embassy in Paris as to whether his hairstyle and beard were acceptable, and he had been assured they were. His pleas fell on deaf ears, and he stood in line with the others waiting to be shorn. It became obvious that the barber was not accustomed to Western clients. One standard cut prevailed for all: above the ears in a "pudding-basin" style! On this occasion, my traveling companion and I were grateful that we were women.

This necessary task accomplished, we were instructed to carry our luggage into the Customs building. There we were presented with a form written in both English and French. We were required to list, first, all valuables we were bringing into Albania; second, all the currency that we had with us; and third, all newspapers, magazines, and written materials in our possession. One sentence was written in bold type at the bottom of the form: "Anyone who fails to answer these questions accurately will be condemned!"

We filled out the forms and waited in separate lines for our luggage to be searched. We had already settled in our minds that if one of us was prevented from entering the land, the other would proceed alone. This was not a happy thought, but for us there was no alternative.

Almost without interest, two officials took our forms and casually rummaged through our cases before returning them to us. There was no attempt made to search our persons or our handbags. Some members of the group had the magazines or novels they had brought with them confiscated, with the promise that they would be returned in Tirana immediately before the group flew home to Paris. Anything that spoke of or illustrated life in the West was regarded as dangerous.

When the entire group had been inspected, we were ushered outside to where an Albanian coach was waiting for us, complete with an Albanian guide. The last requirement was to have a guard compare our faces with the photographs on the group visa. When he was thoroughly satisfied, we boarded the coach. It had taken two hours to complete the formalities.

Gears in reverse, the bus edged toward an impressive pair of gates topped with barbed wire and surely electrified. A soldier appeared, unlocked them, and swung them open. Slowly we moved forward through the gates, which were immediately closed behind us. High electric fences ran parallel to the road for some distance from the border till they merged with a large military barracks. Once past this, we began to gather speed and approached the first small village. Into our hearts came a flood of differing emotions. Albania at last! The impossible had become possible!

CHAPTER TWO

Praying Always—With All Perseverance

In the 1960s, in the green and pleasant land of New Zealand, it was possible to be a Christian and yet be almost totally ignorant of the life and condition of Christian brethren in Communist lands. In 1968, my ignorance was shattered by the visit of a pastor from Eastern Europe, who had spent many years as a prisoner for Christ's sake. Of him it could be truly said that "No name of a crime stood against him but only the crime of a Name." * He spoke not with human eloquence but with the sincere compassion of a man made perfect through suffering.

In the cool of a summer's night, I stood outside the large suburban Baptist church in my city of Auckland, where he had spoken. A curious mixture of thoughts raced through my mind: *What could I ever do to express my love and concern? How deeply committed to the Lordship of Christ was I? Enough to suffer even as these believers were suffering? Why did God allow such things to happen to His people? Why had I had life so easy and they had had it so hard?* And with these many thoughts, many emotions filled my heart. Did I really

---

* Tertullian

care? Would it take only time for me to forget what I had seen and heard this night? Was it the emotion of fear that I felt in my heart? Could it be mixed also with faith?

Yet even in the multitude of my thoughts and feelings, there came a strong conviction that God had spoken in a personal way. My decision to enroll in the School of Evangelism of Youth With A Mission in central Europe for the winter course of 1970 was not made lightly. It had meant resigning from my teaching position in order to spend a minimum of eight months in Europe.

After only a couple of weeks at the school, a new teacher arrived from Holland—Brother Andrew by name. He came as a man with an obvious burden, and he shared in detail the needs and conditions of believers in all of Eastern Europe. But throughout the course of his week's lectures, he would return again and again to speak about the country of Albania. I learned for the first time that, alone in the continent of Europe, this nation of two million people (which served as the setting for Shakespeare's *Twelfth Night*) was dedicated to the principles of communism as expounded by Mao, and that its links were with Red China, which made it as vocal against Russia as it was against the capitalist nations.

The last official census of religious affiliations, taken in 1945, revealed that 70 percent of Albanians were Moslems, 20 percent were Orthodox Christians, and 10 percent were Roman Catholics. Only about 200 Albanians were Jewish, and less than 100 were Protestants. Official hostility to religion after the Communist takeover was concentrated particularly against the Roman Catholic church. Anti-Catholic feeling was boosted by false propaganda put out by the government and widely believed. According to this propaganda, Roman Catholicism first came to Albania during the last war, with the help of Mussolini and the despised Fascists. (In fact, it was brought to the country around 1250 by Franciscan monks.)

Soon after the takeover by the Communists, foreign priests began to be murdered and deported on the grounds of their "Fascist allegiance." This action was followed by systematic killing and imprisonment of native Catholic leaders. The campaign against religion in general was stepped up in February 1967, following a major speech by Party leader Enver Hoxha. The "young generation" stormed the churches and mosques throughout the land; over 2,000 convents, monasteries, mosques, and churches were destroyed or altered to suit "better purposes," such as cultural buildings, theaters, and sports halls.

In the city of Shkodra, for example, youths play basketball beneath the mosaic dome of the former Roman Catholic cathedral, while in the same city the headquarters of the secret police is housed in a former convent. Also in 1967, the country's religious laws were nullified and the practice of religion was strictly forbidden. Priests and ministers were put to "productive" labor. According to official sources, the Christians burned their Bibles and the Moslems their Korans, thus enabling Hoxha to proclaim the "People's Republic of Albania" to be the first atheistic nation on earth.

In September of 1968, it was heard on Radio Tirana (the official Albanian station, named after the country's capital, which broadcasts regularly in many languages throughout Europe) that Christians were still meeting in secret. "But," the announcer added, "we will settle with them." Another broadcast from Radio Tirana stated that there had been only a few Christians fanatical enough to resist the new measures, and severe steps had had to be taken with them. They had been sealed in barrels and rolled into the sea. At the same time, Hoxha declared in front of the Congress of the Democratic Front that the battle against tradition and practiced religion, which was rooted in the conscience of the people, was not yet finished.

On April 23, 1969, the London *Daily Telegraph* printed an announcement given to them by the Vatican. It concerned the execution by firing squad of a Roman Catholic priest, Father Shkurti. With a group of his parishioners, he had fled over the border into Yugoslavia to escape Communist persecution. The Yugoslavs had handed the group back to the Albanian government. The execution had taken place November 26, 1968.

Brother Andrew departed at the end of the week, but he left us with the challenge of this nation uppermost in our minds. Albania was the first country in human history to deny so blatantly the existence of God and to seek so ruthlessly to destroy and suppress every symbol and expression of worship and faith.

What could we do? Only one thing: We could pray! We could give ourselves to God as intercessors for this nation. Two or three times a week when lectures concluded at night, we would gather in small groups of five or six people. Because we were so limited in our knowledge of the people and their needs, we were dependent upon God for revelation and leading as we prayed.

How precious, how powerful, and how true Jeremiah 33:3 became to us: "Call unto me, and I will answer thee, and show thee great and mighty things, which thou knowest not" (KJV). It was as if this nation became our own, and its people our people. We walked its streets; we felt its sorrows and its pain. But we understood also that God was aroused, that He wanted to vindicate His holy Name and to prove not only to this nation but to all nations that the government is still upon His shoulders—that it is impossible to force God out of any land by decree.

One night while our small group was waiting for direction in praying for Albania, God gave me a vision. This was an unusual experience for me, yet it was so simple and clear and direct that I could not doubt it. I meditated on it for some time before sharing it with the other members of the group. Very simply, I had seen four things: myself, a tour bus, a small building, and the face of a woman. (She appeared to be a cleaning woman who had come from scrubbing a bathroom.) With these impressions came the knowledge that I would enter Albania in a bus as a member of a tour group and that I would meet this woman, whom I presumed was an Albanian.

Together we praised the Lord for speaking to us in this way and thanked Him for the miracles He must perform to bring this about. In 1970, Albania was a closed and isolated land; only the Red Chinese had easy access to it. There were no tour groups able to enter it of which we were aware.

In April of 1970, our lecture session being completed, we traveled as a school group on a ten-week field trip through Italy, Yugoslavia, and Greece, to Israel and Turkey, and then back through several Communist lands to Switzerland. Albania was still very much on our hearts—so much so, that when in Belgrade, the capital of Yugoslavia, we located the Albanian Embassy and made inquiries about entering the country as tourists. As we pored over a map of the area, we realized how close we were to the northern Albanian border. Embassy officials, however, were totally unimpressed with our inquiry. They gave us not the slightest glimmer of hope. The answer was very definitely "NO!"

Our first reaction was to remind God of all the hours we had spent in prayer. Most of us had never before in our lives prayed so intently for anything. We needed our wise group leader, Loren

Cunningham, to point out that God is never in a hurry. Our prayers had not been unheard or unanswered. God was at work, and as we continued steadfast in faith and prayer, God would act.

How hard it is to wait patiently for the Lord! And yet as the weeks became months and the months became years, we discovered an important principle: When a burden is given to us from the Lord, it does not lose its strength with the passage of time, but rather gains intensity. In August of 1970, our school concluded, we spread out to different parts of the world. But through our letters and during visits in person, we would share with deep conviction, "We haven't seen the answer to our prayers yet, but we will!" And then we would come again into the presence of the King and lift the people of Albania before Him.

CHAPTER THREE

Though It Linger, Wait for It

In the early months of 1972, I returned to New Zealand for a brief visit. One day, a close friend mentioned that a fellow student of hers at the university had recently accepted a position in Albania. Albania! Surely she must mean Austria or some other European country that began with an *A*! I questioned her further, but there was no mistake. With a degree in political science and a commitment to Maoist communism, this New Zealander had received an appointment to Tirana, the Albanian capital.

So when I left New Zealand in July to return to Europe, I carried with me her name and address and the knowledge that this was another link in the chain that would eventually bring me into the land.

How careful we need to be to distinguish God's movements from His moments. It was not until November 1972, when I was invited to meet a young couple who had returned from ministering in Yugoslavia, that both my head and my heart told me it was time to make my first move. I listened as they shared many details of their trip. But when they told of the feelings that came into their hearts as they drove almost to the Albanian border—and were so close and yet so far from being able to enter it—I felt God nudge me and say, *Now is the time! Write to the New Zealand girl living in Tirana. Tell her you are interested in seeing the land and the people. Ask her if she can help.*

Without delay the letter was written. Within a few weeks the reply came back. It was a warm, yet businesslike letter in which she said she regretted that it was impossible for me to be her guest. However, in the summer of 1973, there would be several tour groups from Europe entering the country, and if I was interested in visiting the land this way, I needed to write to ALBTURIST, the official tourist agency in Tirana. She ended her letter by giving me their address.

As I read, I remembered the impression of the vision during prayer back in 1970: *You will enter the land as a member of the tour group.*

I wrote to ALBTURIST. After some weeks they replied, giving me the names and addresses of three tour groups—one in Switzerland and two in France.

Now that the vision was becoming a reality, I began to think earnestly about a companion. I was convinced that the scriptural pattern was a minimum of two, and I made it a matter of specific prayer. Early in January 1973, a special friend, Evelyn Muggleton, surprised me by saying, "Reona, I've been praying, and I believe I'm to go with you to Albania." Evelyn was one of the few who had been aware of my plans. Had I taken time to sit down and consider who I would most desire to have go with me, Evelyn would have been my choice—but I knew better than to make approaches on a human level.

We had first met in 1971 when we became members of a summer Youth With A Mission team to Afghanistan. Then the next summer, we found ourselves together again on a team in Ethiopia. A deep friendship had developed. So when Evey made her announcement to me, I had to restrain my joy in order to ask solemnly, "Are you sure?" She was sure. So we began to plan and prepare together.

The first tour group to reply was the Swiss agency. It was obviously operating with millionaires in mind! The language used throughout the tour would be German, and there was nothing that appealed to us about it. We waited for the French groups to respond.

One morning a poorly printed little booklet arrived. Across the front cover was written: "Have a Milatant Holiday...Enjoy the Sun and Sea of the Adriatic While We Indoctrinate You." This invitation to join the Young Socialists of France on a tour to Albania did not appeal to us either.

That left only one more group to respond. According to the information we had been able to obtain, the best we could hope for was a reasonably priced tour of seven to ten days, which would take us to a hotel on the coast—probably near the city of Durres—and leave us there to enjoy the sun and the sea and to listen to lectures. Imagine our surprise when the third group responded, offering us a nine-day tour that would take us from the north to the south, to every major city and historic site! The price was reasonable, the language used would be French, and there were two available places. We knew instantly this was the one, and by the end of April 1973, we were confirmed as members of this particular tour that would depart from Paris on June 27 and return there July 5.

Any work for God requires careful preparation. Leafing through our diaries during the early months of 1973, we saw the way God was preparing us. Easter fell during April that year, and during the days prior to it, I was impressed strongly with Psalm 24, particularly the latter verses. The first mail that arrived after Easter brought me a letter from my friend in New Zealand, who, in 1972, had given me the name and address of her acquaintance in Albania. She mentioned that when praying for me, she had been strongly impressed with Psalm 24, particularly verse 7: "Lift up your heads, O gates, and be lifted up, O ancient doors, that the King of glory may come in!" (NASB). She asked, "Is God leading you to go through some ancient doors?" I could not doubt that God was speaking to me through this psalm. I began to read the history of Albania. In a secular book, I found a reference that the apostle Paul had first brought Christianity to the nation. The authors gave Romans 15:19 as their source: "by the power of signs and miracles, through the power of the Spirit. So from Jerusalem all the way around to Illyricum, I have fully proclaimed the gospel of Christ." They pointed out that Illyricum is the ancient name for Albania. Then I understood why God had been underlining this verse. *Those ancient doors had closed, but they would open again and the King of glory would come in.*

Our times of prayer alone and together increased as the months sped by. Spring was loudly announcing its arrival when a Swiss friend urged us to accept her invitation to spend two days in a chalet high in the one of Switzerland's most beautiful cantons. After driving for an hour, we left the car at the village of Les Marecotes, with its shops and chalets clinging to the ledges jutting out from the hillside. Then, because the road was no more, we took a mountain cable car for the last leg of the journey. Skimming the tops of forest giants, we ascended for ten minutes until the cluster of chalets that formed the village of Le Creuzas came into view. Once outside the cable car, speech left us. Rugged, towering mountain peaks hemmed us in on every side, their summits wreathed in snow. A gurgling stream rushed out of the bowels of the nearest hillside in a frantic rush to reach the valley below. Golden buttercups, deep mauve and white clover, blue forget-me-nots, and large white daisies jostled each other in the fields beneath the village. The air was cool and crisp, yet smoke did not rise from any chimney. We were the only occupants of the village. The silence would be broken only by our own laughter or conversation or by the occasional mournful screech of a mountain hawk. For two unfettered days, we feasted at His banqueting table; we knew His banner over us was love.

In early June, I awoke one morning and began to read a psalm—Psalm 23. When I came to verse 4, it was as if I had never read it before: "Yea, though I walk through the valley of the shadow of death, I will fear no evil: for thou art with me; thy rod and thy staff they comfort me" (KJV). I felt as if God were speaking those words personally to me. What could it mean? Quickly I turned to the New Testament. My reading for the day was Luke 21. In the Living Bible, I began to read:

> *There will be a time of special persecution, and you will be dragged into...prisons and before kings and governors for my name's sake. But as a result, the Messiah will be widely known and honored. Therefore, don't be concerned about how to answer the charges against you, for I will give you the right words and such logic that none of your opponents will be able to reply!... And everyone will hate you because you are mine and are called by my name. But not a hair of your head will perish! For if you stand firm, you will win your souls* (verses 12-19).

It was some days before I shared with Evey the weight of those words. Then, together, we committed ourselves into His keeping for whatever lay ahead.

The teacher at the Youth With A Mission school in Switzerland was Ken Wright, an engineer from New Zealand. After an evening lecture that both Evey and I attended, Ken came over to us, knowing nothing of the journey we were about to make. He began to prophesy, "The Lord would say unto you, 'Do not be anxious. Do not have unrest in your hearts. The road ahead of you is not an easy one, but as you walk it, you will not break; you will not crumble.'" After his prayer, he asked us what we planned to do. When we told him, he smiled and said, "I understand."

One further significant event occurred just days before we left for Paris. Many of our friends were leaving to spend the summer in ministry in different lands. We gathered to pray for one another. When it came to our turn, we sensed the presence of God and the power of God as Loren Cunningham prayed a somewhat unusual prayer. He said, "Because of your going into the nation of Albania, I believe there will be a release of God in that land." At the time, none of us fully understood the meaning of that prayer. We were to understand it later.

CHAPTER FOUR

The Gates of Hell Shall Not Prevail

Three years had passed since I had first heard the statement, "The Christians in Albania have burned their Bibles." But it was impossible to forget! I wanted to cry out, "No sincere Christian would ever voluntarily burn his Bible!" The thought of entering the land was always accompanied by the thought of taking in the Word of God in the Albanian language, so that those forced to burn their copies might have again the strength and comfort that the Bible affords to believers. I thought that obtaining the Word of God in Albanian would present no problem.* Bible societies and missions would surely have copies available.

Our first inquiries, however, brought apologetic replies, that regrettably nothing was available. At one stage, it looked as if we would have to go in empty-handed. We made it a matter of specific prayer. One mission which felt sure they had had some Albanian Scriptures but could not locate them then wrote to say they had been found. From another source came a letter saying they had

---

* The Albanian language belongs to the group of Indo-European languages, but forms a branch by itself, being derived from the Illyrian-Thracian tongue.

available a limited number of Gospels of John in Albanian. We rejoiced to receive both these contributions. All told, we received approximately 50 copies of "The Way of Salvation" (a collection of Scripture verses) and 12 copies of the Gospel of John.

We had already learned in our lives that anything vital for God will be tested by the enemy. Therefore, it did not come as a huge surprise when, only a matter of days before we were to depart for Paris, a letter came from the tour group saying that the Albanian Embassy had denied me an entry visa. That New Zealand did not have diplomatic relations with Albania, was the reason given. The letter ended with an interesting sentence: "We are sorry to have to give you this information, but before finally saying you cannot make the trip this summer, a new Consul has been appointed to the Albanian Embassy. He takes up his position this week, and we will refer your application to him."

The work of the enemy was obvious. It was possible to laugh the laugh of faith and to stand resolute and committed to the truth of James 4:7: "Submit yourselves therefore to God. Resist the devil, and he will flee from you" (KJV).

On the twentieth of June, an express letter was delivered. It simply stated: "We are pleased to inform you that your New Zealand passport is acceptable to the Consul for Albania for your proposed visit the 27th of June to the 5th of July. With our best wishes...."

God was at work, and who can withstand Him!

Our passports had been in Paris a full month in order to obtain the Albanian visa. Before we could travel from Switzerland to meet the group in Paris, they needed to be returned to us. Of course, the tour organizers were aware of this. Three days before departure, there was still no sign of our passports. We telexed to Paris. There was no reply. Two days before departure, we telephoned. The mistake had been realized, but it was now too late to send them by post. The only possibility was to give our two passports to a man flying from Paris to Rome, who was to change planes in Geneva. We would both have to come to the Geneva airport to claim our passports from him, or else he would fly on with them to Rome. Again, we recognized the source of the problem.

As we prepared to leave for the airport, I remarked to those in the car, "This is an important journey. If we fail to meet this man and collect our passports, the Albanian trip can be forgotten." I knew we needed to pray before going, and I suggested it weakly, but somehow we started up the engine and were off.

Midway to the airport, traveling at about 90 kilometers an hour, the vehicle without warning came to a grinding halt. There was no time to tinker with it. We were about to have our first exposure to the art of hitchhiking. Praying and attempting to look both professional and distressed at the same time, we were surprised by the speed with which our need was recognized. We were offered a ride, and we arrived at the Geneva airport with time to spare! There was no difficulty locating the man with our passports; the problem was to hitchhike back to our vehicle and get it started. Our attempts brought no response. Finally, it was towed away, never to run again!

It had been an exhausting and frustrating day. There were questions in our minds still requiring answers. We had been aware of the contest in the heavenlies. Were there experiences ahead of us for which we were not prepared?

This little nation of Albania, only 28,748 square kilometers in area, is the second smallest country in Europe. It is situated on the western section of the Greek peninsula and bordered on the northeast by Yugoslavia, on the southeast by Greece, and on the west by the Adriatic and Ionian seas. The forerunners of the present-day Albanians were the Illyrians, who have inhabited Albania since the time of the Bronze Age (beginning approximately 2700 B.C.). During the second half of the third century B.C., they were attacked by Rome, and conflict with the Romans continued for two-and-a-half centuries. The Romans finally conquered Illyria but were not able to subjugate the people, especially those living in the mountain regions. In the fourth century A.D., with the partition of the Roman Empire, the provinces of Albania passed over to the dependence of the Eastern Roman Empire—to Byzantium. But not even as a result of this partition and the subsequent migrations and invasions of the Barbarians (Hues, Goths, Avars, and Slavs) was the ethnic composition of the people of Albania much affected. It was during the eleventh century that the people of the region began to be referred to as Albaneans, after the dominant Illyrian tribe, the Albanes.

At the end of the fourteenth century, the peril of a new conquest threatened: Invading Ottoman hordes poured in from the East. Unable to impose their feudal military domination on the country, the Turks obliged the Albanian nobility to pay them a yearly tribute. When a split developed among the Albanian feudal lords, Venice sent men to occupy the important coastal cities of the land. With the onslaught of the Ottomans and the Venetians, Albania was driven down the road of constant impoverishment until it became the most backward nation of Europe.

Why was this nation, still bearing the stamp of poverty inherited from the past, so important to the enemy? In light of its geographical location was it relevant to consider that, in the tenth chapter of Daniel, two strong princes of darkness are mentioned: the Prince of Persia and the Prince of Greece? Was the apostle Paul trying to enlighten us when he said in the sixth chapter of Ephesians: "For our struggle is not against flesh and blood, but against the rulers, against the authorities, against the powers of this dark world and against the spiritual forces of evil in the heavenly realms" (verse 12, NIV).

Were we coming against a particular stronghold of the enemy? Could this be the explanation behind the extraordinary measures this nation had taken to suppress every vestige of religion? Is this why on every tombstone in the land the cross has been replaced with a red star? Is this why over 2,100 churches, convents, mosques, and other religious institutions have been utterly destroyed? Is this why care is taken to speak about "the second century before our era"—never "the second century before Christ"?

Chapter Five

Go Through, Go Through the Gates

The drive from Switzerland to Paris in the early hours of the morning was pleasant and fast. With more good fortune than skill, we wound our way through the center of Paris and arrived at Le Bourget Airport an hour earlier than expected. The place appeared deserted, and we soon found a notice saying our plane had been delayed for two hours.

After some time, people began arriving. More than once we had wondered aloud what the other 18 members of our group would be like. "Who," we mused, "would want to spend his vacation in Albania?" As members of the group entered the terminal building, we were not disappointed. They appeared to be interesting people. Almost exclusively French-speaking and French in nationality, they ranged in age from a retired couple in their mid-sixties to a young 17-year-old economics student from Paris' prestigious Science Po. Restrained introductions seemed to be the order of the day.

To our delight, we found that the tour leader spoke English. When we began to question him about Albania, we were surprised to learn that he had never been there before either. He assured us, however, that at the border we would be joined by an Albanian guide for the duration of the tour. It soon became obvious, too, that on our flight to Dubrovnik we were going to be accompanied by a second group, whose destination was also Albania. In marked contrast to our party, they were all young people, scruffy in appearance, and extremely vocal—the "Young Socialists of France," off to enjoy their militant holiday in the sun!

Our passage through French Customs was a mere formality. But as we entered Passport Control, we were surprised to find a member of our group offer a British passport. We had noticed her immediately when she entered the airport. She looked approachable, so when the bus was driving out to our Yugoslavian Airlines plane, we introduced ourselves.

With a minimum of delay, we were airborne. Europe was sweltering under a heat wave as we flew through a cloudless sky, enjoying the panorama of the French, the Swiss, and the Italian Alps. Then the rugged majesty of the Yugoslavian coastline came into view, and we made our descent to the coastal city of Dubrovnik. Here the airport appeared strangely deserted. It remained that way for two hours, until a bus arrived to take us over the mountains to a hotel in Trebinje. It was hard to understand why we needed to drive for an hour—over 25 kilometers of narrow mountain roads—to rest for the night, when Dubrovnik was blessed with an abundance of hotels. But we asked no questions and were given no explanation.

In the information that the group had sent us, it had been made clear that we would be accommodated two persons to a room. Therefore, when a little after ten at night we reached our hotel and were ushered into the reception area to be given our room numbers, we were surprised to find that we were to be three to a room. The woman with the British passport was to join us. The following day, we would cross the border and enter the nation of Albania. (In times of prayer as we prepared for the trip, we had brought this first night many times before the Lord. In Europe we had asked the few who knew what to expect at the border, and all had agreed it would be simple and straightforward. No search would be made of our luggage or person. It might be time-consuming, as there would be forms to fill out, but we would surely have no problems entering. Our problems would begin once in the land. Still, we planned to spend time seeking the Lord together. Now that would be impossible! It was hard to accept the situation. Could God have made a mistake?)

We ate a late meal and returned to our room. It was almost midnight, and the obvious thing to do was to sleep. With heavy hearts, Evey and I prepared for bed. The light went out. Then our British friend, Mary,* began to talk.

"You know, I have been here before; six years ago, in fact. It's going to be interesting to see how the country has changed. We can expect to have fun at the border tomorrow afternoon. It took us six hours to get through last time. They make a really thorough search of all luggage. It's literature they are primarily concerned with."

Evey and I were glad that it was dark, lest the color that had suddenly flooded our faces be detected. Our British friend talked on. The thought of sleep seemed to have left her. She filled our heads with such useful and interesting information that it was frustrating not to be able to write it all down for future reference. She recounted that on her previous trip two Italian members of the group were refused entrance at the border. No reason was given other than that they were classified as undesirables. In the course of the tour, two members were interrogated—one because he had taken too many photographs and the other because he had wandered too far along the Durres beach on his own. At one point, children had begun to throw stones at them, and in the face of such treatment, Mary was not surprised that British tour groups to Albania had ceased to operate. (We were to learn later that our British friend was a journalist with a famous newspaper, assigned to compare the present Albania with the one she had visited six years before.) God had not made a mistake. He never does make mistakes. In His love and mercy, He was getting the information to us we so badly needed!

Sometime after midnight, I heard Evey ask a question: "Mary, do you think many wildflowers grow in Yugoslavia?"

Our friend replied that she imagined so. Evey went on to explain: "Reona and I have an interest in wildflowers, and this will be our only chance to gather some in this country. Let's set the alarm for six and take a walk early tomorrow morning and see if we can collect some for pressing."

I quickly agreed that this was an excellent idea. Mary muttered something about sleep being more important than wildflowers. The alarm was set, and with joy and thankfulness we slept!

---

* Mary was not her real name.

With the sounding of the alarm, we were awake, out of bed, and dressed on double-quick time. Noiselessly, we made our way out of the hotel and out of the village until we found a quiet and secluded spot by a river. Out came our New Testaments, and we read and prayed individually and then came together to commit the day to God.

The memory of that scene by the river is still etched in my mind: the rustic beauty of the countryside, the gentle warmth of the sun; but far more precious, the presence of the Son of God as we poured out our hearts to Him. We worshiped Him in the beauty and stillness of that place; we allowed Him to search our hearts, should anything break our fellowship with Him that day; we rejoiced in the cleansing power of the blood of Christ; we yielded to the control of the Holy Spirit; and then we began to obey the command of Ephesians 6, to put on the armor of God. (This was no special act of preparation because of the challenge of the day, but something that had for several years been a vital part of our daily walk with the Lord.)

Into both our hearts at the same time, God began to say an identical thing: *Today you will be literally clothed with the Word of God as you enter this nation.* Our feet were to be shod with the preparation of the gospel of peace. The fact that both of us were wearing clogs simplified this process. It was possible to fit two Gospels of John under each foot and still walk comfortably. Similarly, the girdle of truth and the breastplate of righteousness took on new meaning for us that day! Midsummer weather meant that we would be most uncomfortable dressed this way throughout the day. According to our itinerary, we would have a stop for lunch when only an hour from the border; therefore, we planned to take advantage of this time to "put on our armor." In this way, we were able to account for the greater part of the literature. A little would still be in our suitcases and shoulder bags. Before returning to the hotel, we gathered wildflowers and had quite an impressive display to show Mary when we met at breakfast.

We traveled again the mountain roads to Dubrovnik—often referred to as "the city of a million secrets." We were given an hour to wander at will through this ancient walled city. Tourists from many lands were clattering cheerfully up and down the worn and patined stones of the Placa—surely one of the most beautifully preserved high (main) streets in the world. For years, Dubrovnik was a free republic—and a small one, too! It is possible to do the complete two-kilometer walk around the walls—walls which contain a perfect microcosm of history from medieval to renaissance to gothic to baroque.

It was fascinating, too, to plunge from one of the broad squares into the network of alleys which make up the city. There was always something new and fascinating to catch your attention: "raznici" (pork or veal kabobs) sizzling on pavement barbecues; hawkers, with large trays of colorful leather work, anxiously seeking to give us the best bargain in town; and beautifully embroidered tops and skirts swaying tantalizingly in the breeze outside grubby, dark bazaars.

The hour passed all too quickly. Regretfully, we returned to the bus. Leaving the city behind, we drove through fields of pomegranates and olive trees. Then, as we continued south, we began to traverse the craggy pine-clad coast of the Dalmation Riviera until we reached the international youth hostel at Budva, where lunch was served to us.

We boarded the bus again, our destination being Hani Hotit—one of two possible border crossings into Albania. Both entries are from Yugoslavia. The second one is much farther to the south and east, at Qafa e Thanes.

Chapter Six

Do Not Fear What They Fear

Exclamations of praise to God come quickly and naturally to the lips of Christians. We realized that it would be less than wise to speak this way while on the tour, even if few in the group understood English. We had agreed, therefore, to use the word *marvelous* when we wanted to say "Praise the Lord," or some phrase like it. As our bus began the drive toward the city of Shkodra, many members of the group were still smarting from the humiliating new hairstyle they had been made to acquire or the baggy pair of poorly made jeans they were forced to wear—and several were being quite vocal about it. We could only look at each other and say, "Marvelous!"—and we really meant it!

There was beauty to be seen in the countryside. Barley, maize, and wheat were ripening in the fields. Proud sunflowers were reaching tall to the heavens. Extensive tobacco plantations stretched to the distant foothills. The trees were heavy with fruit, and terraced vineyards climbed the mountainsides. In the early evening light, the hills were a mixture of blues and soft purples. The fields were filled with workers—mainly women—hoeing and weeding and gathering in the grain. Only a few were making their way home, yet it was already early evening. The surface of the road was surprisingly good, but driving was hazardous as bicycles competed with ox- and donkey-drawn carts, and groups of sheep and cows endeavored to claim the right-of-way.

According to our itinerary, we would spend the night at Shkodra. This is the principal city and the most important economic and cultural center of northern Albania. It was also the ancient capital of Illyricum. Indeed, it is one of the most ancient cities of Europe, having been occupied by the Romans and the Byzantines. The ruins of the ancient Illyrian Fortress of Rozefat dominate the city. Today it has a population of 49,000. Our itinerary promised us a rapid tour of the city to be followed by a visit to the museum, to a children's hospital, and to a copper-wire factory the following day. Evey, being a nurse, had looked forward to the hospital visit. But alas, it was not to be.

We entered the city at about 6:30 P.M. and stopped outside a modern hotel. The only disconcerting feature was that it appeared to be closed. After about ten minutes, our guide returned looking flustered and told us we were free to walk in the city for half an hour. This brought murmurs from the group, but Evey and I were conscious of a miracle taking place. We had been told by Christian workers that for the duration of the tour, we would be under the closest scrutiny and that there would be no freedom to do anything independently of the whole group. To emphasize the point, we were told the story of a young European who had entered Albania with a tour group previously. He, too, had brought with him Scriptures in the Albanian language and, as we intended to do, had left them at various places throughout the land. As he was about to leave the country, he was met by an official who handed back to him every portion he had given out. He was then taken from the group, driven to the border, declared *persona non grata*, and left there to find his own way back to northern Europe. Now we were being told to walk anywhere in the city—virtually to do our own thing for half an hour! Had a new attitude arisen toward tourists, or was God so ordering the circumstances that this freedom was a special gift from Him?

We had made friends fast among the group, and when we stepped off the bus, we were joined by Mary and a French woman. Excitement filled our hearts—our first opportunity to walk in the streets and to be among the people! We were not, however, prepared for what was to follow. Even in our conservative dress, we were easily identified as tourists. As we left the bus and walked toward a busy street, the people began to back away and then, from a distance, to stare at us—a mixture of fear and hostility in their eyes. In spite of this attitude, they were an attractive people. Many of the older women were in national dress (long peasant skirts with full-sleeved bodices and black waistcoats), while the younger women were conspicuous by their bright-red lipstick.

Children, with their natural curiosity, did not know enough to withdraw, and shyly they would come toward us. Immediately, adults nearby would call them. If there was no response from the children, they would drag them back with force. This was a new and painful experience for us. In a small measure, we had a sense of what it must have been like to be a leper in ancient times and to have society withdraw with the cry, "Unclean! Unclean!" Was it going to be like this for the eight days we would be in the land?

We left the busy street and wandered through a park made beautiful by the oleander bushes in full bloom. Here, mothers were pushing their babies in high-wheeled carriages, but our smiles at them and their children were not returned. A man with a very ancient camera was busy arranging a group: a proud grandmother, a mother, and her child of about a year old. At his command, they smiled broadly, and the scene was captured.

And then the unexpected occurred: As the four of us stood by a monument to Lenin, an elderly peasant lady emerged from the group of adults who had withdrawn and were silently observing us. She came first to Evey. She shook both her hands, embraced her warmly, and then began to speak in Albanian. She did the same thing to me and then melted again into the crowd. Our two friends remarked on how strange it was that she would have done such a thing, and then only to the two of us! We were silent as we made our way back to the bus. God was emphasizing that in the most impossible situations He is at work. We were convinced that the dear Albanian lady was a servant of the Lord, who had sensed we, too, belonged to His family. Had we been able to convey His love to her? In the future, we decided, we must not be caught with the other group members, as this limited us in the way we could respond.

Once back at the bus, we learned that the hotel was indeed closed. None of the efforts of our guide to have it opened for us had been successful. This meant we would be driving on through the night to the coastal city of Durres. There would be no tour of the city, no visit to the museum, hospital, or factory. Again there were angry murmurs from the group. We could only reflect on the experiences of the past half hour. What exciting encounters with people did God have ahead of us? If need be, could we even speak with these people in their own language?

Fortunately, never again were we to encounter such fear and hostility from the people. To the contrary, we found them warm and loving and easy to approach. Surely it must be that in this northern city, so close to the frontier, special efforts to indoctrinate and instill fear in the hearts of the people had been undertaken, lest they contemplate the possibility of escape.

Darkness overtook us as we drove directly south. Frequently, our bus would slow down to make room for little groups of people, with farming tools over their shoulders, who were wending their way home.

Without warning, the bus stopped. We were told to get out. Many thoughts raced through our minds. Had we been discovered so soon? In Shkodra, we had gratefully visited a restroom and transferred the literature to our shoulder bags. Mine was a particularly good one. I had bought it in Egypt the summer before. Only after I had owned it for several days did I discover that it had not two compartments but four—two underneath as well as the two obvious ones on either side. However, our fears were unjustified. There was a natural explanation. A serious pig disease in the land caused a situation in which every vehicle had to be stopped at regular intervals and made to drive over a pile of straw that had been soaked in a strong, evil-smelling disinfectant.*

We were required also to walk across the straw. This was no problem for us with our clogs, but many of the group resented the indignity of it and the damage done to their expensive shoes. This performance happened not once, but several times during our drive to Durres.

Another significant experience occurred at this time. We were not at all sleepy, so when it became too dark to watch the countryside slipping by, we talked quietly, reviewing the events of the day. Not once but three times in the space of about one-and-a-half hours, we found ourselves about to say identical things to each other. When it happens once, it can be passed off as coincidence, but not when it occurs three times! We had prayed much for unity—the unity that the Bible speaks of. Although two persons, we had prayed that we might be like one: one in thought, in heart, and in action. Now we seemed to understand on the first evening in Albania that God had answered our prayers. This was, in fact, amply demonstrated in the days ahead.

Durres at last! We drove through the city and on to the coast where several tourist hotels had been built, all in a row and all identical. Ours was the first in the row. By night, it looked quite impressive. All of us soon located our rooms. This time, two to a room was the order. We gratefully received our key and visited our room. Then, even though it was 10:30, a good meal was served. Since the tables were set for four, we had on this occasion the pleasure of the company of our Albanian and French guides. We noticed that the waitresses were all young teenage girls, and our Albanian guide explained that they were "volunteers" who were happy to work without pay during their summer school break.

We returned to our room with a multitude of thoughts in our minds and great expectancy in our hearts.

---

* In 1973, there were only about 2000 vehicles in the land—mostly buses and trucks used for industrial and agricultural purposes. There were no privately owned vehicles.

CHAPTER SEVEN

They Shall Hear My Voice

The sun, streaming in the balcony window, awakened us. To our shame, we found it was ten minutes after eight, and breakfast had already been served in the hotel. Our group was to assemble at ten in the lounge, so this gave us time to take a walk and see our surroundings in the light of day. We went first to the impressive Adriatica Hotel. Whereas our hotel and the others that belonged to our row were set back from the beach, the Adriatica fronted it. There we were able to change our money into Albanian leks,* and this gave us an excuse to inspect the reception and dining rooms. We also discovered a shop on the ground floor that sold good maps of the country, as well as books in several languages summarizing the history and present progress of the nation. To our surprise, a booklet entitled "Handbook of English-Albanian Conversation" was also available. Its contents included the Albanian alphabet and a guide to its pronunciation, a small vocabulary, and conversation for general use. The foreword explained that ALBTURIST had compiled the book to help foreign visitors to Albania explain what they want, ask questions, and make requests. We gratefully bought these items.

* One lek is equal to approximately 30 cents American.

After this, we wandered out onto the terrace. In front of us, a host of bodies stretched out on the yellow-white sand, and even at this early hour, a few hardy souls had ventured into the surf. Few of these sunbathers were tourists—almost all were Albanians, apart from small groups of Chinese, easily distinguished by their uniform blue swimming shorts and by the fact that they stayed together in groups of about a dozen.

By any standards, it was a magnificent beach. Albania is fortunate to have over 400 kilometers of coastline. This gives the country not only beautiful beaches and adequate port facilities, but also enormous fishing reserves. We made a quick inspection of the shopping area, which consisted of several rows of kiosks, there to serve the holiday population. (The city proper is about ten kilometers away.) We sampled a bottle of soft drink (having noted it was sealed). It lacked the coldness of refrigeration, but its taste was good. There was nothing else to tempt us. Tomatoes, cucumbers, and onions were the sole produce at the greengrocer's kiosk. In another, the bread—enormous loaves of it—looked nutritious and, by the smell issuing forth, was freshly baked.

We continued to satisfy our curiosity by peering into windows, when we heard the sound of children singing. Two by two, like the animals in Noah's ark, they marched past us, keeping time with the military beat of the song they sang. They appeared to range in age from 5 to 12 years. They were uniform in two respects: All wore plastic sandals, and all had red scarves around their necks. We later learned that there were several "Pioneer Camps" for children in the area—provided, of course, by the State.

When we assembled as a group in the lounge, our Albanian guide, profuse with apologies, explained that there had been some alterations to our itinerary. Today we would be having a double treat. In the morning, we would drive to the mountains northeast of Durres to the town of Kruja, some 46 kilometers away. This town of 6,000 people had become famous because it was the birthplace of Scanderberg, the national hero of Albania. Scanderberg, whose real name was Gjwegji Kastriot, was born in 1405 of noble parents. In 1423, his father gave him to the Turks (who had conquered the land) as an act of submission and proof of loyalty, and he stayed in the palace of the sultans. In 1438, he returned to Albania and became the governor of Kruja. From this position, he began to make plans for a military insurrection. In 1443, he left the Turkish army at a time when they were preoccupied with heavy fighting against the Hungarians, and from the city of Kruja he proclaimed the restoration of the principality of Albania. His flag—red with a black double-headed eagle imprinted on it—flew above his fortress. For 24 years, he successfully dealt with every renewed Turkish assault, repelling them all. Only after his death in 1468 did Albania find itself again under the Ottoman yoke. This time the yoke would remain until the twentieth century.

At Kruja, we would visit the fortress and Scanderberg Museum. In the afternoon, we would drive through to Tirana, since 1920 the capital city of the land. There we would tour the National Liberation Museum, the Palace of Culture, and Scanderberg Square. Again there were murmurs from the group because, according to our itinerary, we were to have spent a full day in Tirana. Now it had been reduced to a few hours!

As we left the coastal plain, the road began to ascend a series of hills and elevations. The higher we climbed, the more beautiful became the landscape. Olive tree plantations and limestone rocks, limestone quarries and limekilns predominated. We were told that stones from these quarries had been used for centuries to build towns and cities. The olive trees were old also, dating from most ancient times. Legend has it that Scanderberg decreed that no young man could marry before having planted 20 olive trees.

As we climbed yet still higher into the mountains, the glare from the limestone hills and the white-coated cement buildings was intense. Upon entering Kruja, our bus deposited us outside a modern hotel. The view was outstanding. The mountain of Kruja towered above us. At its base, an equestrian monument of Scanderberg had been erected. It gave the impression that he was just about to assault the enemies that were besieging his fortress.

The fortress to the east of the town loomed like an enormous warship anchored to a huge mass of solid rock, semidetached from the mountain. Today almost nothing remains, however, of the original fortress that Scanderberg built. We walked first to the museum, which is dedicated to the struggle of the Albanian people against invaders. Groups of children followed us, and we discovered that the older ones had begun to study English and were able to speak and understand a few words. We did not progress much beyond "What is your name?" "My name is…" and "How are you?" or "I am very well, thank you." So out came our handbook of English-Albanian conversation. It was fun, and I was sorry when we reached the museum and the lecture began. The museum contained many historical and literary works, portraits, and sketches. But my heart was with the children, and after some time, I escaped to find them sitting in a little group patiently waiting outside the door. I began to mention names they would know: Lenin, Marx, Hoxha, Scanderberg. Then, pointing to the heavens, I said, "Jesus." There was no recognition, just a puzzled look on their faces as they shook their heads. It was hard to keep back the tears; 65 percent of the present population know nothing other than communism. "How shall they believe in him of whom they have not heard? and how shall they hear without a preacher?" (Romans 10:14, KJV).

A real effort had been made to preserve the antiquity of the town. We walked back through a narrow cobbled street with wooden chalet-type buildings jutting out so far that their roofs almost formed a canopy overhead. It had once been a typical medieval bazaar. Lunch was served at the hotel, but we returned to the older part of town to enjoy Turkish coffee served at low tables or on the carpeted floor, as we preferred.

The drive to Tirana, which is situated almost in the center of the country, took us a little over an hour. There our bus parked in Scanderberg Square, the impressive center of the city. The square is flanked on either side by wide, tree-lined streets and is dominated by monuments to Scanderberg and Lenin.

We were scheduled to go first to the Palace of Culture. Again, with apologies, our guide told us that this was not going to be possible, so we visited the National Liberation Museum. An enthusiastic lecturer began to tell us the history of the nation. The gist was that the Albanian people are among the most ancient inhabitants of the Balkan Peninsula. From antiquity to the twentieth century, they have come into contact with ten civilizations, experiencing from them military bondage, massacres, arson, and devastation. Their history has been a sad story of never-completed occupations and never-decisive uprisings. Greeks, Romans, Turks, and, more recently, Italians and Germans have all invaded this tiny land. Throughout these ruthless clashes, the Albanians have incurred enormous losses, but they have never been annihilated. On the contrary, when the whole of Europe shuddered before the Ottoman menace, the Albanians, under the leadership of Scanderberg, nailed down the Asian giant for more than a quarter of a century and wrote pages with their blood in the history of Europe.

In 1878, when Bismarck declared at the Berlin Congress that there was no Albanian nation, the Albanians took up arms and compelled him to reckon with them. To the end, he remained hostile, but he no longer dared to claim that there was no Albanian nation. Even at the beginning of this century, as the Turkish historians themselves admit, the Albanians were the first people to deal heavy blows to the empire of the sultans, now vanished in history.

The achievements that have been recently attained are considerable. Albania of the wooden plow, of the oil lamp, and of massive illiteracy* has become a country where medical treatment is free of charge, where one in every three persons attends school, and where all people under the age of 50 are literate; a country of collective and partly mechanized agriculture; a country preparing to turn out its own iron and steel and to put into operation one of the biggest hydroelectric power plants in the Balkans.

With these stirring words ringing in our ears, our guide surprised us with the announcement that we now had two hours to walk in the city. We didn't wait to be told twice. Tirana, although a relatively young city, has a population in excess of 229,000 and is responsible for one-third of the nation's total industrial output. Many of its buildings are modern, and there are several parks in the area. We made our way to the biggest of these, recognizing it would be an excellent place to leave behind the Word of God—on benches, the tops of hedges, or the walls of a fountain.

Many times we acted independently as we saw the opportunity arise; other times we would be a team, one doing the watching or distracting attention while the other deposited the booklet. We had discussed several times how important it would be to trust each other totally and not to question the wisdom of what had been suggested. It related again to the question of unity. We were rank amateurs. We had never done anything like this before, yet available to us (according to the promise of James 1:5) were liberal amounts of God's wisdom. Daily we saw this divine wisdom in operation in each other. It was never the case of one always being the leader and the other always the follower. On the contrary, it seemed that on one day Evey would be getting the impression of what to do and how to do it, and the next day it would be reversed. We found this both relaxing and exciting.

* In 1940, 80 percent of the nation was illiterate.

We walked back from the park along the wide main street. What a different scene from the capital cities of other lands. Few vehicles passed by, just an occasional bus or taxi or a car belonging to a diplomatic mission—that was all. Comparatively few people were visible either. As we came to an intersection, Evey noticed two young men standing in front of a soft-drink kiosk. One stood out by the tailored cut of his clothing, and Evey said, "I believe we are to speak to him." We came up casually, and Evey began the conversation in French. Immediately the young man in Western-style clothes replied in impeccable French. He gave us his name and explained that he had spent time outside of Albania. It was difficult to conceal our wonder and amazement. Our guide had already told us that less than five percent of the population are permitted to ever leave the country, yet God had led us to one of this privileged percentage, and we spoke a common language! His friend spoke only Albanian and so became a silent listener. Evey, whose French is far superior to mine, began like any curious tourist to question him about the land and the people and to show a real interest in the answers he gave. He let us know that he wanted the conversation to continue, even to the point of buying us both cool drinks.

After about ten minutes of talking, in my role as the praying partner, I longed that the conversation might come around to spiritual things. As I looked out across the city, my eyes lingered on the elaborate dome of a beautiful mosque—one of the most exquisite monuments of nineteenth-century architecture. The Mosque of Haxhi Ethem-Bay has not been demolished because of the value of its architecture. I began to think that mention of this building might be the way to enter into the subject. As I thought and prayed, Evey turned to me and asked if there was something I wanted to say. Before I had time to reply, I saw her turn toward the mosque and begin to question the young man about it and about matters of religion in general. He gave the answers one would expect from a loyal young Maoist, stating that religion was no longer a part of their society and that Albanians did not believe in God. All this time, his friend, though not understanding the language, was listening intently, searching our faces and seeking to interpret the conversation.

Then I heard Evey begin to talk with great boldness about the person of Jesus Christ—about the fact that she enjoyed a personal relationship with Him. I held my breath and prayed all the more fervently. He was content to let her do most of the talking.

Occasionally, he would comment with a seemingly neutral statement. We checked the time and realized we needed to be back at the bus. Evey explained this, and then I heard her say, looking into the eyes of the young man, "...you may forget almost everything I have shared with you this afternoon, but never forget that Jesus loves you and that He died for you." With no change in the tone of his voice but looking directly back at Evey, he replied, "Je le sais et je le crois." ("I know it and I believe it.")

Then we understood that our conversation had been with a believer, a brother in Christ. Wisely, he had given his friend no reason to become suspicious by the tone of his conversation. We returned to the bus elated in spirit.

Our group was waiting patiently, but there was just one problem. The driver was missing. With a gleam in her eye, Evey suggested that we have our photographs taken at the foot of a huge statue of Lenin situated near our bus. We gave our cameras to a girl in the group, who needed to go back some distance because of the height of the statue. As we sat down, Evey carefully withdrew a Gospel from her pocket and passed it to me. As we continued to pose, it was possible to push it behind us until it lay at the giant's feet. With wonderful timing, the driver appeared, our cameras were returned, and we became the last of the group to climb into the bus. The word *marvelous* came readily to our lips as we pulled away. The gospel, the power of God unto salvation, lay at the feet of Nikolai Vladimir Lenin, the one who finished his life uttering these words:

> I have made a great mistake. Our main purpose was to give freedom to multitudes of oppressed people. But our method of action has created worse evil and horrible massacres. You know that my deadly nightmare is to feel that I am lost in an ocean of blood coming from innumerable victims. It is too late to turn now, but in order to save our country, Russia, we should have ten men like Francis of Assisi. With ten such men, we would have saved Russia.*

On our drive out of the capital city, we made a brief stop to view the Reception Palace which, as the name suggests, is the place where visiting dignitaries are received. Then the buildings of the

---

* Last words of Russian Bolshevik leader, Lenin, quoted in Catholic Quote, October 1968.

university were pointed out to us. Many of the group were vitally interested in the question of education and were therefore given a host of impressive facts and statistics. Today the population of Albania is twice that of 1923 and 70 percent larger than in the year 1945. This is the result of an increasing birthrate and decreasing death rate. The average life span of an Albanian is now 65 years, in comparison with 1938 when it was 38 years. Over 42 percent of the population is under 14 years old. In 1938, Albania had only 650 schools with fewer than 60,000 pupils. Only 1,600 students attended secondary schools, and 61 students pursued higher studies abroad.

In 1972, an official report stated that three-quarters of a million people (that is, 38 percent of the population) were involved in education—725,000 students and approximately 29,000 teachers and lecturers. Eighth-grade education is compulsory for all. Of these 725,000, 50,000 are young children attending kindergarten or preschool. Preschool education for children three to six years has been established throughout the whole country, including the most remote villages. Its objectives are twofold: to rear healthy, active children ready to begin school, and at the same time to create facilities for more mothers to participate in productive work and social activities. The parents pay 40 percent of the expenses for the maintenance of their children at the kindergarten, while the State pays the remaining 60 percent in Albania today, a worker has an average of eight years' schooling, while one-seventh have been through secondary and higher institutes of learning. In addition to the University of Tirana, the Upper Institute of Agriculture, the Upper Institute of Arts, and the teacher training institutes, there were, in 1972, about 25 central institutes and stations engaged in research work in social, technological, and natural sciences. Over 28,000 students were in attendance. Sixty percent of these were workers who pursue their studies in part-time schools. In recent years, priority has been given to the training of workers specializing in agriculture and animal husbandry and in the industrial extracting and processing of minerals and primary materials—for deposits of pyrite, copper, chromium, coal, ferronickel, phosphorite, rock salt, marble, and asbestos are being mined. Indeed, Albania supplies close to one-eighth of the world's copper. She also has substantial oil deposits. One of the major industries in the land is the production of chemical fertilizers. It has been estimated that in 1975, production will have increased 77 percent over that of 1970, reaching the 330,000-ton mark.

By the time we reached our hotel at Durres, most of the group were ready to have dinner and retire for the evening. It was Mary who suggested that the night was still young and that a walk along the beach would be refreshing. Daily we marveled at the schedule, or rather the lack of it, that we were obliged to follow. Our hotel was never officially closed for the night. We came in and went out as we pleased. There was no suggestion of being followed or of observers placed in strategic places to watch our movements. We had been so conditioned to expect the suspension of all personal freedom that it took some time to relax and take full advantage of the situation.

We were a foursome as we kicked off our sandals and enjoyed the coolness of the evening sand beneath our feet. About a quarter of a mile away, a pier jutted out into the sea, and we could hear music coming from it. Although it did not sound very Albanian in flavor, we decided to investigate. Crowded into a very rudimentary structure were people of all ages and sizes. At the far end, a band was effectively drowning out the sounds of conversation, and the narrow space around them was being used by some of the younger set to stomp and sway.

Many eyes fastened upon us as we searched for a vacant table. No matter what we wore or how effectively we kept our mouths closed, we always seemed to have our label showing saying, "Made in the West."

Everyone around us appeared to be drinking something different, so, using our faithful "English-Albanian" phrase book, we decided to order lemonade. There was no hesitation from the waiter when we made our order. He reappeared bearing a tray with tall glasses filled with a dark liquid. "Lemonade?" we asked. "Yes, yes" was the reply. Gingerly we sipped a mouthful—prune juice was the general consensus.

It was refreshing to be in the midst of something authentic and not staged for the benefit of our tour group. We left regretfully around midnight, but no one else appeared to be thinking of following our example. For them, their two-week holiday at the beach was a time to be treasured and enjoyed to the fullest. Hadn't they worked long hours, six days a week, 50 weeks of the year, to qualify for this bonus?

CHAPTER EIGHT

The Earth Is the Lord's and Everything in It

Saturday, the thirtieth of June

In contrast to the day before, we woke early. According to our itinerary, we were to spend the day in the city of Durres and its environs. This included a visit to an archaeological museum and to a Roman amphitheater now being excavated. In the afternoon, we were to visit the State farm at Sukhti—a farm particularly famous for the cereals and fruits raised year-round. We left immediately after breakfast and drove along the coast to the center of the city. Durres, an ancient city founded in 627 B.C., is the principal port. With a population of 52,000, it is the second-largest city in the land.

Our first visit was to the mausoleum—an impressive new building approached by a series of graded steps and dominated by the inscription, "Glory to the Martyrs." Again an enthusiastic lecturer met us and guided us from one martyr's grave to the next for about 30 minutes. From there we drove to a massive site, more than 120 meters in diameter, where a Roman amphitheater built at the beginning of the second century A.D. is being excavated. The work is proceeding slowly, however, because, as our guide explained, "The people whose homes we demolish must first be rehoused." Assistance is being given by the Archaeological Institute of the Academy of Sciences of the People's Republic of China.

Two levels beneath the ground level of the amphitheater, the remains of a Byzantine chapel built in the tenth century in the subterranean vaults and foundations of the amphitheater have been excavated. We were taken to this section last and shown a polychrome mosaic mural which is still intact today. The pulpit and the altar area were clearly visible, and we lingered at the spot, praying silently. When our group had moved on, Evey and I sang together the chorus:

He is Lord, He is Lord,
He is risen from the dead and He is Lord.
Every knee shall bow, every tongue confess
That Jesus Christ is Lord.

After placing a copy of the Gospel of John on the altar, we thanked God that although the gates of hell assault the church, they will not prevail. God has built and will continue to build His church in this land!

The archaeological museum was nearby. It is one of the richest museums in the country. Throughout Albania's history, invaders who stayed some time left marks of their culture behind, and the country is rich in wonderful archaeological treasures. Outstanding among them is a collection of ceramic kitchen utensils, unearthed at a necropolis belonging to a period when the city had close ties with the city center of Magna Graecia. The museum also has a rich collection of tombstones. These are important because the Illyrian names inscribed in sepulchral stones reveal the ethnic composition of the people. On the portico next to the museum are sculptures, pillars, cornices, capitals, and altars. It is not hard to imagine what magnificent buildings used to embellish the city in ancient times. We would like to have lingered much longer here, but we were moved on to the Culture Palace—a recently completed building which has, in addition to the big hall of the theater, numerous minor halls and studios for various cultural activities. When the foundations were being laid for this building, the ruins of ancient thermal baths were discovered. When the palace was completed, these ruins were reconstructed. The morning had passed quickly, and we were taken back to the hotel for lunch.

The State farm at Sukhti was only a few kilometers from our hotel. We found that several other tour groups were visiting there the same afternoon. We listened first to an extensive lecture describing the concept of collective farming to which Albanians adhere:

> Albania is a mountainous country. Almost one-third of the total area is over 6,000 feet high. Its climate is Mediterranean, with hot, dry summers and rain concentrated in the cold season. Fortunately, rivers and streams abound, providing both irrigation for the fields and hydroelectric power. The countryside constantly demands your attention. The terraced hillsides, the fields crisscrossed with irrigation ditches, the mountains reforested to their highest peaks—all bear testimony to the enormous collective effort put forward by the people in the area of agriculture.
>
> More and more throughout the nation, the Socialist concept of farming is practiced. Agriculture forms the basis of the national economy. Since the liberation of the country, production has increased fourfold. The area of cultivated land has tripled, much of this new land resulting from the reclamation of marshy areas, once hotbeds of malaria-carrying mosquitoes. Vast improvements have occurred in the cultivation of grapes, olives, and other fruits, while new crops like tobacco, cotton, and sugar beets have been introduced. Mechanization of farming began after liberation. In 1938, there were only 38 tractors in the land; by 1968, the number had risen to 10,000. Much effort has been devoted to the production of electricity, so that now even remote villages have this available to them. There is no doubt in the minds of the people that socialized collectivization of agriculture has proved enormously superior to private enterprise farming.
>
> Two basic forms of farm management are practiced: Agricultural cooperatives and State farms. The cooperatives consist of the voluntary union of landowning farmers who have chosen to give their buildings, land, materials, and labor for the good of the people. Ninety-nine percent of the land is now managed collectively, and private ownership is virtually nonexistent. At first, each member of the cooperative was given a house and a portion of ground for personal use, but as the social conscience was raised, this custom was discontinued.

Each member of the cooperative receives payment in money and produce, and each cooperative aims at being self-sufficient. The surplus is sold to the State, and all profits are returned to the cooperative and reinvested in it. The members assume full responsibility for decisions and have the right to elect or to be elected to an office in the cooperative. The supreme authority is the General Assembly of all member cooperatives.

The State farms are extensive areas of land owned and operated by the national government. They aim at efficient mechanization which will result in a high level of productivity. Again, each worker is salaried and receives the equivalent of a worker in a factory, thus insuring equality between industry and agriculture. In 1972, the salary was 600 leks a month (approximately 180 dollars). In 1973, there were 32 State farms spread throughout the country. Harmony exists between the State farms and the cooperatives, with new seeds, superior breeds of animals, and other materials being shared and compared. Where possible, the size of each State farm is being increased as more land is reclaimed. In 1944, a typical farm covered an area of 400 hectares.

By 1973, it covered 10,000 hectares. Prior to 1944, its only vehicles were four tractors; now it uses 200 tractors, 40 harvesting machines, and 30 trucks. Thirteen thousand people live on this one farm. Of this number, 4,000 work directly on the farm, while the rest consist of family members, soldiers, and students. The farm is divided into ten sections, and each section has its own housing units, farm buildings, a school that covers eight grades, and social institutions such as a hospital, a cultural center, and a nursery. (Nurseries care for babies up to nine months. The mother is freed to spend two hours each day with her baby. Then, at nine months, the babies are placed in central preschools; and at three years, they are transferred to kindergartens. These all function at night also, so that mothers can do shift work when required.) In addition, on the farm are five middle schools, one secondary school, and a branch of the university.

It was disappointing to find that instead of being given a conducted tour of the whole establishment, we were taken only to one area, where tomatoes were grown and packaged. The fields of ripe tomatoes were extensive, as was the packing shed. Crates were stacked floor to ceiling, and girls with pieces of cloth tied around their heads were sitting on boxes grading tomatoes, according to their size, into different crates. We were told that these were for export and that the large trailer trucks we had seen entering and leaving the country at the border contained either potatoes or tomatoes bound for France or Germany. A large red-and-white sign was being pasted on the boxes: ALBANISES ERZEUGNIS ("Albanian produce"). The drivers of these trucks are among the five percent who leave the country. Two are assigned to each truck, and behind the seat is an area for sleeping. This enables them to spell-off each other as they drive to their destination and return again, stopping only to refuel. These drivers are married men with children. Their return to the country, therefore, is virtually guaranteed.

Many within the group had considered that the visit to the State farm would be one of the highlights of the tour. Therefore, it was disappointing to be told that we were returning to the hotel to listen to a lecture given by a leading editor. We were to attend this with other French-speaking tourists. We would be encouraged to ask questions at the conclusion of the address. Much of the content of the speech had to do with the political objectives and structure of the Working Party of the People. The editor told us that the Party's objective is to create the new man—and the new man is its greatest achievement. To fully understand the accomplishments of the Party, he felt we needed to know a little of its history:

> In the early years of the twentieth century, the Ottoman Empire began to crumble. Finally, after the First World War, Albania's independence was recognized internationally. A series of princes (and then in 1928 a king—Zogu, by name) held leadership in the nation. They leaned heavily upon other governments for investment and economic aid, and under King Zogu, the nation was virtually ruled from Rome. Then in 1939, the Fascist army of Italy invaded and conquered the land. King Zogu fled, leaving behind a defeated and betrayed people. On the twentieth of October, 1941, a clandestine meeting was attended by leaders of resistance groups from all over the nation. As a result, in November 1941, the Communist Party of Albania was formed. All true patriots, without political or religious distinction, were welcomed to join this Resistance Army in the struggle against the Fascist oppressors. By 1942, the Party

numbered 10,000 men. In 1943, the situation improved, and the majority of the large cities were liberated by the Army. On the tenth of July, 1943, Spiro Moisiu became the commander of the National Liberation Army; his political adviser was Enver Hoxha.

On the eighth of September, 1943, Italy was defeated; Albania was then occupied by the Nazis. By the end of 1943, the Resistance Army numbered 20,000 men, with groups in even the remotest towns and villages. Despite German massacres, the People's Army remained strong. On the twenty-fourth of May, 1944, 200 delegates attended a conference at Permeti. There a provisionary government was created, led by Enver Hoxha. (Hoxha—whose name means "Moslem priest"—was born at Gjirokaster on the sixteenth of October, 1908. He received his higher education in Korca and then went to France and to Belgium, first as a student and then as a worker. He returned to Albania in 1936 and became a teacher at a school in Korca. He held this position from 1937 to 1939. In April of 1939, he was removed from his teaching position by the government in collaboration with the Italians. He went to Tirana and immediately joined the Revolutionary Force.)

Reinforced by an additional 70,000 men, the Resistance Army began the last offensive against the Germans in June 1944. Five months of bloody fighting ensued. The last battle was fought in Tirana, where it raged for 19 days. On the twenty-ninth of November, 1944, Albania was entirely freed. During the period 1939-1944, 100,000 men were involved in the People's Army. Of that, 28,000—that is, 2 1/2 percent of the population—perished in the struggle. Another 80,000 were imprisoned during this time. Thirty-seven percent of the dwellings in the land were destroyed, and the overall damage done to the country was estimated at 1.6 billion dollars. Mines, forests, highways, and bridges were almost entirely destroyed.

On the eleventh of January, 1946, the People's Republic of Albania was proclaimed and a constitution was approved by the Assembly.

Until 1960, the country collaborated closely with Russia. But then a divorce took place, and Albania assumed responsibility for its own development. The Party is based on the fundamental principles of Marxism-Leninism, on the revolutionary experience of the country, and on the specific conditions of

> development in Albania. However, the Yugoslavs have a saying, "When it rains in China, the Albanians put up their umbrellas." It is true that a great deal of the progress being made results from Chinese aid. Many of the factories and power stations have been built with Chinese funds, with Chinese equipment, by Chinese technicians. Numerous posters are displayed in the streets praising Chinese-Albanian friendship. Historically a fiercely independent people, the Albanians resent any suggestion of Chinese influence in their country, and they staunchly maintain that Chinese aid is available without interest. In recent years, diplomatic relations have been established by Albania with over 30 nations, but still not with Russia.

The lecture and the question-and-answer period continued until after nine in the evening. We were free to leave if we so desired, and many did so. A wide variety of questions were asked, and in several sensitive areas, inconclusive answers were given.

After a late meal, Mary invited us to walk and talk. We reviewed the day together. Early in the morning, Mary had taken a walk on the beach. To her surprise, she had found a young boy there able to speak good English. This encouraged her to speak to children more frequently—and in English rather than French. She also began to talk about some of the changes that had taken place in the land since her visit six years before. In 1967, she had been unable to find any adults wearing watches; now many adults possessed them. Then, only foreigners wore clothes made of patterned material; now it was in evidence in the cotton garments worn by adults and children alike. It had been impossible then to buy a postcard, even in the most expensive hotels. Now there was an abundance of beautiful cards at all hotels and in many kiosks.

Retiring to our hotel, we eagerly looked forward to what the new day would hold in store for us.

Chapter Nine

This Is the Day the Lord Has Made

Surprisingly, Sunday is a day of rest in Albania. Breakfast was served an hour later, and once again our official itinerary was put aside with the announcement that the morning would be free and that a visit to the beach was recommended. We used the first part of the morning to read and pray and to worship and praise our God together. There was so much to be thankful for, and Evey and I rejoiced at His detailed leading and provision. My psalm for the day was Psalm 86, and I read:

> Bend down and hear my prayer, O Lord, and answer me,
> for I am deep in trouble.
> Protect me from death, for I try to follow all your laws.
> Save me, for I am serving you and trusting you....
> Listen closely to my prayer, O God. Hear my urgent cry.
> I will call to you whenever trouble strikes, and you will help me.
> Where among the heathen gods is there a god like you?
> Where are their miracles?
> All the nations—and you made each one—will come and bow before you, Lord, and praise your great and holy name.

> For you are great, and do great miracles.
> You alone are God....
> O God, proud and insolent men defy me; violent, godless men are trying to kill me.
> But you are merciful and gentle, Lord, slow in getting angry, full of constant lovingkindness and of truth; so look down in pity and grant strength to your servant and save me.
> Send me a sign of your favor. When those who hate me see it they will lose face because you help and comfort me (TLB).

The beach then beckoned us, and we enjoyed the sun and the sea for a couple of hours. It was not difficult to distinguish the tourists from the Albanians. The latter wore an identical cut of swimsuit. Two-piece costumes were worn by all the women and girls, which seemed strangely out of keeping with the conservative standards of dress generally adhered to. Quite close to us, a group of Chinese were endeavoring to acquire a suntan. They kept strictly to themselves, but we were to see them again later at the dining room of our hotel.

Our hotel was never more than one-third full, and frequently other parties joined us for meals. We had just received our customary first course of soup when the blue-suited Chinese began to enter. We gave up counting after 70 (the group was in excess of 100), and when they were seated, a screen was drawn between us. Their entry caused a considerable stir among our group, and we began to realize that several members had a particular interest in the activity and influence of the Chinese in the land.

During lunch, a delegation approached our Albanian guide and asked him what was planned for the afternoon. When he said that nothing was planned, they reacted strongly, so he calmed them down by promising to arrange something. We were to assemble again at two o'clock. True to his word, he had arranged a boat trip that would take us to the Port of Durres and then out some distance from the shore before returning us to the pier. The thought of this was less than exciting, and the older members of the group declined the offer.

The rest of us set off on the kilometer walk along the beach to where the boat was to meet us. We noticed other tourists were walking with us; the same offer had been made to all the groups staying in the area. We reached the pier, but it was boatless. After about 30 minutes, we noticed a rather ancient vessel laboring toward us. It looked as if some considerable time back it may have been a naval patrol boat. A wind had risen during the afternoon, making the sea quite choppy. There was a mad scramble to get on board, and a few decided at this point to walk back along the beach rather than share a seat with several others or cling precariously to some piece of the superstructure just for the sake of taking an Albanian boat ride.

We headed for the Port of Durres. In spite of requests from the group to visit the port the day we were in the city, our guide had said this was not possible. Now we were to view it from a different angle. Its size had deceived us. As we approached from the sea, we realized facilities, including a shipyard for repairing Albania's commercial fleet. Maddeningly though, as we would approach one pier closely enough to begin to see the name and the home nation of the ship (without exception they appeared to be Chinese), our boat would veer away and head out to sea. In all innocence, Evey and I decided to change our position on the boat and climbed a stairway to the upper deck. To get out of the wind and spray, we edged our way around the funnel. There to our surprise was a member of our group with the most sophisticated camera equipment, training his telephoto lens on the disappearing ships! Confusion and embarrassment were written all over his face, and he muttered something about the sea becoming rough. (From the beginning of the tour, we had had a "gentleman's agreement" with several members of the group: "Don't ask me why I have come to Albania, and I won't ask you." When friendships had been established, we promised one another *to tell all* on the plane flight home.)

By the time we had left the Port of Durres behind and were heading out toward the open sea, seasickness had overcome several, so the captain was prevailed upon to bring us home a little ahead of schedule. On our walk back to the hotel, I found myself beside the English-speaking Albanian guide of the Norwegian group who were accommodated in the hotel next to us. She was a schoolteacher who "volunteered" her services in this way each summer. She explained that professional people were required to be involved in other aspects of life, and that if she were not a tour guide, she would be required to spend some time each year working in a factory or on a farm. Comrade Enver Hoxha had instructed that "intellectuals should be plain and unpretentious, just as the people (of the) working class are unpretentious. They should follow the example set by the working class and be as loyal…to the great cause of the people, prepared for sacrifice." We talked together about schoolteaching as we had experienced in our two countries, and when we parted to our respective hotels, she wished me an enjoyable stay in her land. Neither of us knew that, within 24 hours, we would meet again under radically changed circumstances.

It being too early for supper, Mary joined us, and we walked in the opposite direction along the beach. We had been told that in this area the holiday homes for the workers were to be found. Fronting the beach were numerous rest and recreation camps for schoolchildren and working people. A little further on was the safe swimming area; here were numerous small cabins and cottages, each one crowded with people. Many were sitting on the front steps, welcoming the relief that the sea breeze brought.

As we passed one cabin, a woman sat in her doorway spinning carpet yarn. We stopped and smiled, and she returned the smile. We lingered, and she beckoned for us to come closer. Out came our trusted phrase book, and with its aid we learned a little about herself and her family. How we longed to be able to openly give her a Gospel of John, but we had already considered the situation and decided that daily we would seek to be as wise as serpents, yet as harmless as doves, leaving behind the Word only when opportunity presented itself. Then, if we still had many booklets remaining, on our last evening we would blanket the beach area where so many people were crowded together.

Sunday was truly proving to be a day of rest. Nothing was planned for the evening. During supper Mary said, "Wouldn't it be fun to go into Durres tonight? I'm sure the city will be crowded with people—since this is their one day of rest—and we could mingle with them without being so obviously tourists. It's the group that always gives us away."

How to do this was the problem, but Mary was not one to let problems remain unsolved. She had already discovered that the staff in our hotel did not understand English. Whatever you asked them, they always replied with the answer "yes." Mary therefore said, "You know, if I asked the staff at the hotel if we could go to Durres, I know they would say yes. That would be official permission, and then we could catch a bus into town and spend several hours in the city."

We told Mary we were willing to join her if she obtained permission. She approached the woman behind the desk and politely asked to go to Durres. With no hesitation, the woman replied, "Yes." We also invited Hélène, the youngest member of our group, who also was Mary's roommate, to join us. We had discovered the bus stop some days previously, and so we set off as a foursome. We experienced no difficulty catching the bus. It was crowded, but we slowly worked our way toward the back. Try as we would to look Albanian, we did not succeed. The first shy stares, however, quickly changed to warm smiles. They were a friendly people and, even without language, warmth and love were conveyed. The contrast between our first encounter with the Albanian people in the northern city of Shkodra and the undisguised friendliness of all encounters after that only served to emphasize the grim measures that must have been taken to guard against escape.

Having already seen parts of the city by day, we felt at home when the bus deposited us at the central station. As Mary had thought, the streets were filled with people who appeared not to be going anywhere in particular. We walked along the seafront and then began to follow the crowds up a busy main street. We were grateful that our pockets bulged with Scripture portions, for this was the perfect opportunity to leave many behind—in the bus, at the park, beside the bus station, on the ledges of major buildings. Under the cover of twilight, our primary concern was to be about our Father's business. Our two friends walking with us were blissfully unaware of our activities. Again this demonstrated the unity God had established. Just a nudge on the arm was sufficient to get the message and deposit a booklet. Our attention was drawn to the only kind of advertising permitted in the land: banners, posters, and slogans printed on the sides of buildings, erected in large red letters on boards in every public place (sometimes even illuminated). They were of two sorts: in praise of the Party, such as "Long Live Marxism-Leninism," or "Long Live Enver Hoxha"; or they were directed to the people, "Fight Indifference—Two Hours at Work Is Not Two Hours of Work."

Our feet began to tell us it was time to find a café, preferably as authentically Albanian as possible. Throughout the evening, we had heard the strains of folk music being played. Following the sound of the music, we arrived at a small park. Tables had been set out under the trees. The band played and the people relaxed. We found a table and ordered lemonade. A glass of dark-brown liquid was served—prune juice again!

By now it was 11 o'clock. It was time to locate the bus station and return to our hotel. After a short wait, the bus arrived. It was far less crowded on the return journey. Both going and coming in the bus, we were able to leave behind the Word of God.

Once back at the beach, we took a new route to the hotel and discovered a series of large display boards. A street lamp burned above them. On each board were handwritten letters accompanied by photographs and illustrations. These puzzled us, but again, Mary came to our aid. She explained that these were "Flet Ruffe." To our ears, it sounded like "flat roofs," so we begged her to explain further. She told us that the people of Albania are encouraged to put in writing criticism of any subject or person. This must be presented in written form, and great importance is laid on the neatness and quality of presentation. Photographs, illustrations, maps, and diagrams are encouraged. These are then fastened to large boards. These boards abound throughout the country. Every factory, collective, and State farm has its own. In addition, they are scattered throughout cities, towns, and villages. Even here at the holiday resort was a large one. "Flet Ruffe" can be of two kinds: praise or criticism. The one that we stood looking at was a praise board. Large photographs of selected workers in the hotels were displayed, with statements of their deeds which had furthered the cause of the People's Republic of Albania.

These boards are taken very seriously, as they well should be. Anyone whose name appears on a criticism board has three days in which to reply to the criticism. He is able to acknowledge it and repent publicly, or he can reject it and give his reasons for doing so. If he rejects it, his case is brought before a committee of responsible citizens. If they find him guilty, various measures will be taken; and as a last resort, he will be expelled from his work. All members of Albanian society, regardless of social position, are liable to be criticized. It is possible for a worker to criticize his employer, a student his teacher, a patient his doctor; indeed, this is encouraged.

Examples that we saw included a worker who was criticized by his fellow workers because he did not attend a union meeting. Another criticized the administration of a particular factory, stating that the tools used were not adequate to produce a high standard of work. A third sheet on a criticism board accused a girl of wearing her skirts too short. An illustration accompanied the criticism, showing two girls, one with correct length, one with the skirt level above the knee. In the official tourist guidebook to Albania, the last paragraph in the section on dressing reads: "Tourists should see to it that they are properly dressed, particularly in towns. It is not permitted to walk about in a bathing suit. Women should avoid wearing mini-skirts or exaggeratedly deep decolletes!"

The existence of these boards permits everyone to express himself freely without being intimidated by status. Our guide told us that it was not rare for an engineer or a director of a factory to be demoted because of criticism from one of his workers. It is believed that this is an efficient way to guard against bureaucracy. The slogan is commonly quoted, "When the mass does not control, the bureaucracy takes over."

With the chilling thought of what it must be like to live in such a society—never sure when one's name may appear on such a board—we made our way back to the hotel. As we had expected, there was no one in the lobby of our hotel to question our movements.

I had been aware for some time that I was feeling less than normal, and I began to wonder whether it related to the "lemonade" we had enjoyed at the café. I questioned the other three. They were feeling normal. By the time I reached our room, I knew that I was not well. Perhaps a night's sleep was all that I needed. But this was not to be. Sleep was far from me as I wrestled with a physical condition more severe than anything I had ever experienced before. I knew better than just to grin and bear it. I began to ask God some important and specific questions. Was this an attack of the enemy? Had I grieved the Lord—and, in love, was He drawing my attention to this fact? (I have always found that when my body begins to suffer, I get earnest very quickly with the Lord.) Was this God's way of trying to teach me something new that I needed to learn? Evey was sleeping soundly. While in between frequent trips to the bathroom, I began to realize how much I was looking forward to the next two days of the tour.

We were to leave early on Monday morning for an excursion to the southeast part of the country. We would travel first to Elbasan and Pogradec. Between these two cities, we would inspect the construction of the railway line that was being built by the "Young Volunteers" to link the city of Elbasan with the mining center of Prenjas. Traveling further south to the city of Korca, we would visit a textile factory, the cemetery of the martyrs, and the museum. In order to do all this, we would spend the night at Korca and travel back to Durres on Tuesday. Was I prepared to forgo this trip? Could our lives be more effectively used if Evey went alone and I remained behind and spent the two days in prayer? In the early hours of the morning, I committed my way to the Lord, confident in the knowledge that as I trusted Him, He would act. The discomfort and frequent attacks of pain did not subside, but I was at peace in the knowledge that He was in control.

Chapter Ten

Appointed to Death

Evey woke just before seven. Propping her head in her hands, she looked over at me and said, "Are you feeling all right? You look awful!" I told her I felt awful and that it had been a long night. Being a well-trained professional, she had slept soundly and was totally unaware of my discomfort. However, there was nothing she could have done, and she needed to sleep in order to be strong for the solo assignment that was about to be hers.

I was still unsure of exactly what God was asking of me. So we prayed together and, like Gideon, I put out a fleece: If in the next 30 minutes I had no recurrence of pain or discomfort, I would take it as a green light to attempt the two-day tour. If, on the other hand, my condition was unchanged, I would understand I needed to remain at the hotel.

During the next 30 minutes, there were frequent spasms of pain. Therefore, I accepted my condition and asked Evey to explain the situation at breakfast. This she did. When she returned to gather her belongings for the two-day expedition, we realized what a closely knit team we had become and how difficult it was for us to contemplate separation even for two days. Several of the group came to say how sorry they were that I had to remain behind. Mary gave me some tablets that she was sure would help, and the guide relayed a message that he had left instructions with the hotel staff to take good care of me.

The group departed early, and I began to make up for some of the sleep I had missed the night before. I was dozing lightly when, at about 11 o'clock, a knock at the door caused me to respond, more asleep than awake, with "Come in." I heard the rattle of cutlery, and a member of the hotel staff entered and placed a tray of food by my bed. (I had asked Evey to be very firm when explaining the fact that I was not interested in food and unable to eat it. But I had already learned that the Albanians equate hospitality with food. Several times members of the group had not felt hungry and had declined a particular course on the menu. The waitress would then bring another type of food, thinking they disliked the first that was offered to them. It was very difficult to convey the fact that it was lack of hunger, not lack of enjoyment of food, that was the problem.)

The smell of salami and highly spiced soup did nothing for my queasy stomach, but I turned to smile at the woman who had brought the tray. As I did this, I realized I was looking into the face of the woman whom God had shown me in the vision while I was praying in a small group in 1970! My heart began to pound, and I prayed to God to give me time so that I would know what to do. About one o'clock there was another knock at the door. I said, "Come in." The same woman entered, bearing yet another tray of food. She put it beside the untouched first tray, and then she did an unusual thing. She sat down on my bed, took both my hands in hers, and just looked into my eyes. I knew what I must say. Slowly and with fervency, I said, "Marx, Lenin—No! Jesus—Yes!" Tears came to her eyes, and leaning over she embraced me and said in very limited English, "Me Christian, too!" I gave her a copy of the Gospel of John. She began to read a verse out loud, then she laughed and cried at the same time. After a few minutes, she reluctantly slipped it into the pocket of her black uniform, picked up the first tray, and left the room to continue her cleaning duties in the hotel.

I fully expected her to return, so when at four in the afternoon there was a loud knock at the door, I called out, "Come in!" In came a man of about 50. In broken French he said he was from ALB-TURIST and I must come with him. At first I thought I was not hearing properly, so I asked him to repeat the sentence. I had heard correctly the first time. I explained that I was ill and could not come with him. He replied that he would wait outside while I put on a coat, but I must go with him. He scarcely gave me time to find my clogs and slip on a dressing gown before he opened the door and beckoned me to follow him.

Down the long corridors of the hotel we went until we came to Room 201. I am sure there was a rise in my temperature and a quickening in my pulse as I walked down the corridor seeking to take in what was happening. But many times during the early days of the tour, I had remembered the words God had quickened and the understanding that He had given—that the road ahead was not an easy one—and I had wondered just how it was going to come to pass.

He pushed open the door of a small room, in which were crowded five men. Three sat behind a table. The windows were closed, and the air was already blue with smoke. They pointed to a chair directly in front of the table, and I sat down. It became obvious very quickly that the men in the room performed different functions. One was an interpreter, one was to act as a scribe to record all the proceedings, one was the official from ALBTURIST, and three had come through that afternoon from Tirana to conduct the interrogation. These three were members of the Ministry of the Interior.

They began by asking straightforward questions: name, nationality, occupation. They presumed that because I was with a French group, French was my mother tongue. I hastened to explain that this was not so and that I needed an English interpreter. This displeased them and forced a temporary halt in the proceedings. The French interpreter left, and in his place came the English-speaking guide from the Norwegian group. She was a temporary replacement until an official interpreter could come through from Tirana.

Her eyes grew wide when she saw I was the accused, and she said coldly, "I don't believe you could do such a foolish thing!"

We began again. After the preliminary questions, a copy of the Gospel of John was placed on the table and the chief interrogator, a man in his early forties, asked me if I had ever seen it before. I replied that I had seen one like it, if not it. He then said, "Your friends have exposed you." I asked him which friends he meant, and he said, "Your friends in the tour group." I told him that was impossible. I had only one friend in the group, and she would never expose me because she loved me.

Into my mind flashed the incident that had occurred in an East European country during the past decade. Several pastors in a town were arrested simultaneously and brought in separately for interrogation. Each one was told that another pastor in his town had exposed him. One after the other, their reply to their interrogators was identical: "That could not be so. That pastor is my brother. He loves me. He would never expose me." When all had been interrogated, the man responsible for their arrest said, "How is it possible to have such love and loyalty? I want what these men have." The memory of this story brought strength and comfort to my heart.

With a cynical sneer, the chief interrogator said, "Don't talk to us about love. What is it anyway?"

It must be remembered that the entire interrogation had to be interpreted—the interrogator's questions from Albanian into English and my answers from English into Albanian. Without further reference to my friends in the group, one of the men said, "The person you gave this booklet to exposed you."

To this I had no immediate answer, but in the following days I was to receive understanding. There was little doubt in my mind that the Gospel that lay on the table was the one I had only a few hours earlier given to the hotel worker. Was she a Judas? Had she really betrayed me? I was never able to believe this. Her subsequent behavior reinforced my conviction that she was a true believer, my sister in Christ.

Several times in the next two days she came to my room, weeping quietly, and just hugged me, taking my hands in hers and squeezing them tightly. Because the room was now bugged, she knew better than to say anything. I had also to remember that it was God who first showed me her face and gave me to understand that I would meet her. What actually did happen only eternity will reveal. In her joy and excitement did she show it to another hotel worker? Did it fall out of her pocket? Did she leave it lying about somewhere? Was it discovered in her uniform pocket when she changed her clothes?

With considerable restraint and gentleness, the chief then urged me to answer their questions simply and honestly. "If you tell us the truth, no harm will come to you."

I told him that would not be a problem as I was accustomed to telling the truth. The questions now concerned where I had obtained the literature and how it had been brought into the country. I realized they were clever men, phrasing their questions in order to trap me. I began to think carefully about my replies. This angered them, and to my surprise, one of them began to glare at me and shout, "Liar! Traitor!"

It was then that God flooded my mind with the words from Luke 21: *Don't be concerned about how to answer....I will give you the right words and such logic that none of your opponents will be able to reply!* (TLB) From this moment, I ceased to labor with my own mind and began to prove the truth of the promise. What peace of heart and mind resulted!

Without warning, their gentle approach ceased, and they began to demonstrate great anger. The chief thumped the table and roared like a lion while his friend, the one who had shouted, "Liar! Traitor!" left his chair and came over to me until his nose was almost touching mine. He proceeded to babble in Albanian, combining much spitting with his talking. Normally, such treatment would have made me afraid, but the louder and angrier they became, the more peace flooded my being. I could not understand it. At the same time, instead of feeling repulsion for these angry men, I felt genuine, deep love in my heart for them. The louder they shouted, the softer and more gentle my replies became. It really was possible to love your enemies and to bless them that curse you, to pray for them who despitefully use you and persecute you!

When their display of anger did not produce the desired results, they tried a third technique. The chief began by pointing to me and talking at length to the others in the room, obviously about me. At intervals, they would throw their heads back and laugh heartily. None of this conversation was interpreted. It must have continued for some 15 minutes. During this time my spirit was not disturbed. There was so much "liquid love" in my heart for them, I consciously had to restrain myself from smiling back at them. I understood for the first time why there are so many injunctions in Scripture not to fear—to be not afraid for, true to His promise, God was holding my right hand. He was helping me. His perfect love was casting out all fear.

The Communist interrogators aim to do one thing: to make you afraid. When they produce fear in the heart of a victim, they have secured a major victory, for fear paralyzes and destroys. Nothing worries them more than to find their various techniques not producing the desired result. It was possible to read this in their faces; it angered them, frustrated them, and worried them. In an outburst of anger, the chief had exclaimed, "You will be here a long time. You are not cooperating! We will keep you here until you break!" "*...until you break!*" These were his exact words. Then I remembered the Word of the Lord that Ken Wright had brought: "*You will not break; you will not crumble.*"

It was now early evening, and by this time they were leaving the room one at a time, presumably to eat and gain new strength for the attack. Physically, I was weak; I had not eaten in 24 hours. But what was this inner strength I was so conscious of? My mind was alert, my heart was at peace. How gloriously true—"When I am weak, then I am strong!" At this point, the English-speaking interpreter from Tirana arrived, and the tour guide was relieved to be able to return to her group. She gave me a long, searching look as she left the room. Her replacement was a young man in his late twenties. The questioning continued. What had made me come to Albania and do such a thing? Did I not know that no one in Albania believed in God? Did I not know that the Bible was a forbidden book in the land? Who had sent me on this mission?

There was a knock at the door. In came a photographer complete with an impressive array of ancient equipment. The flash attachment was huge. Following orders from the chief, he began to take a series of photographs. Attired in my dressing gown and clogs, I was required to sit, to stand, to walk. I was then photographed with the interrogators, then with the interpreter. This surely was going to be front-page news in the *Tirana Daily*! This took some time, and then the questioning resumed.

Another knock at the door interrupted proceedings. Two poorly dressed men entered. They appeared to be nervous and afraid. After some introductory conversation, the chief pointed at me and asked them a question. They both nodded their heads affirmatively. The chief then asked me if I had seen the men before. When I told him I had not, he seemed to ignore my answer and went on to say: "These are the men who witnessed your crime; as a result of their testimony, you are condemned."

It was difficult to believe these things were really happening. To me it seemed more like a pantomime than an official interrogation. Just as these two witnesses had appeared to be totally mystified by what was happening and very afraid, the scribe was also having difficulties. He seemed to be the most uneducated man in the room.

Instead of an impressive pad on which to record the proceedings, he had an odd collection of pieces of paper, and his one pen refused several times to write. At one point, he leaned over toward me and with sign language asked if I had a pen that he could borrow. On another occasion, they stopped and asked him to read back what had just been said. He was so far behind, it was impossible for him to oblige. He then became the target of their anger.

It was now past midnight, and the interrogators were showing signs of fatigue. Of the three men, one had been strangely reserved and quiet throughout the proceedings. His opinion was obviously valued, as he was always brought into the discussions. Unlike the other two, he had a kind, gentle expression and a real softness about his manner. Many times, following a question, he would lower his gaze so as not to look directly at me. I felt convinced that my Christian testimony was not falling on deaf ears. When the beads of perspiration stood out on my forehead, the gentle interrogator suggested they bring water and let me wash my face. Water was also brought for me to drink.

They had a consultation together, and then, with considerable dramatic effect, the chief began to ask me, "Do you have a father?"

"No," I replied. "He is dead."

"Do you have a mother?"

"Yes."

"Do you have a brother?"

"Yes."

"Do you have a sister?"

"Yes."

"Do you love them?"

"I love them very much."

There was a considerable pause....

Then the chief said, "You will never see them again. You are a traitor to the glorious People's Republic of Albania, and traitors are shot. We will come for you at nine tomorrow morning."

I heard what they said, but again there was no disturbance within my spirit.

Then the chief looked at me curiously and asked, "Did you understand what I said?"

I could only reply, "Yes, I understood what you said. You said that you would come at nine tomorrow morning and shoot me!"

There was a long silence. God chose this moment to imprint a verse of Scripture on my mind and heart. Throughout the following hours and days, it would flash its truth to me like a highly charged neon sign. If I myself had chosen a verse to sustain me through this time, I don't believe it would have been this one. But God chose it for me—and in His infinite wisdom, He knew what I needed most. It was the first phrase of Psalm 31:15: "My times are in thy hand" (KJV).

It was 1:00 A.M. We had been in this stuffy little place for nine hours. They led me back to my room. They went to my suitcase and turned it upside down. Then they stripped the beds, poked large needles into the mattress, pulled everything out of the closet, and took my handbag and emptied out the contents of the two side pockets. They took possession of whatever portions of Scripture they found, including my English New Testament and my *Daily Light*. Surprisingly, one of the interrogators produced a sheet of tissue paper and carefully wrapped all the Scriptures in it.

Feeling that it had been a job well done, they moved to the door. The chief was the last to leave. He simply said, "We know that you are an agent from the Vatican. If only you would confess to this, we would not have to shoot you." I'm sure my mouth dropped open with amazement. At the time, I did not understand how they could imagine such a thing. Only later did I learn that the Christians who resisted, even unto death, the measures to remove every vestige of religion from the land were members of the Roman Catholic Church. Just months before we entered the country, in a labor camp, a priest had been found secretly administering the sacrament of baptism to a baby brought to him by its mother. He was shot at a public execution. The news reached the ears of the pope, and one of Italy's major newspapers printed the story with the request from the pope to Catholics worldwide to pray for the church in Albania, which he called "the church of silence."

Anyone who would do such a fanatical thing as I had done must surely be a Catholic. This must have been the reasoning of the interrogators. I reminded them that they had urged me to speak the truth and that I was truthfully telling them I had no connections whatsoever with the Vatican or with the Catholic Church. "Then we will see you at nine tomorrow" were the chief's last words. He closed the door behind him.

I now knew what a ransacked room looked like. I dropped to my knees beside my disheveled bed and began to pray, "Lord, I believe I need to sleep. You promise in Your Word that you give Your beloved sleep, and I believe that in this situation I am beloved by You. Thank You for the gift of sleep." I then moved all my belongings off the bed to the floor, found a sheet, pulled it over me, and lay down. Sleep came immediately.

CHAPTER ELEVEN

Fear None of Those Things Which Thou Shalt Suffer

Tuesday, the second of July

The hotel was strangely quiet, but then I was its only occupant. It was seven o'clock. I had slept for almost six hours. The first thought in my mind upon waking was, *They will not come for you at nine. They will come much later in the day. This is part of their psychological warfare. You have much time to prepare.* Only God could bring such understanding.

I first restored order to the room. Then, still feeling physically weak, I lay down on the bed and began to say aloud certain Scriptures that I could remember. I meditated on them and then made them the substance of prayer. Earlier during the night, just after the interrogators had left my room, I heard the noise of a cord being dropped along the ceiling and considerable activity going on in the room above me. Everything pointed to the fact that a listening device had been planted. I wanted to give them something to listen to, so after meditation and prayer, I began to sing the many precious Scriptures in song that I had learned. Oh, how they ministered life to my soul, even as I sang!

If this was to be my last day on earth, how should I spend it? Would this be the day of my entry into the presence of the King of kings? Then what should I be doing to prepare to meet Him? I discovered what a realist God is. He seemed to be asking me, *What is it that you will find difficult to leave behind?* I thought seriously about this, and then I realized what a blessed individual I was. I had so few possessions—none of them would be hard to part with. God had allowed me to remain single in order to serve Him more effectively. There would not be the pain of parting from a husband or children.

What, then, would be difficult? Just leaving behind my family and friends. At that moment I understood why the Lord Jesus, as He hung upon the cross, looked toward His beloved mother, Mary, a widow, and said to John, "Behold your mother." And to Mary, "Behold your son." For I felt God saying to me, *Give them to Me one by one, these that you love, and I will take care of them.* I began with the most difficult: my widowed mother. Then I went on to the other members of my family; then to my most precious friends. Having done this, I experienced a release of spirit and heart and mind that was totally new to me. Such joy and praise welled up within me, and I found myself saying out loud: "Lord Jesus, it will be a privilege to lay down my life for You. You are more precious to me than houses or brethren, or sisters or father or mother, or husband or children or lands." In this way the morning passed into the afternoon.

I was resting quietly when, without warning, I became conscious of an evil presence in the room. Into my mind flashed a direct and urgent question: *How important are you to God that He should rescue you out of this situation? What have you ever done for Him and for His kingdom to warrant being released?* There was only one possible answer: "*I* have not done anything to deserve His favor!"

Then came a second question: *Those friends who promised to pray for you—are they keeping their promise? You've agreed many times to pray for people, and you have not always done it. And if they are praying, are they like you so often are—too lazy to be led by the Holy Spirit in prayer?* I could only reply, "I don't know. I don't know whether they are praying. I don't know whether they are in touch with my situation."

I found these questions and the answers that followed exceedingly painful. Then it was that God came to my rescue. Into my mind flashed another precious and powerful truth—one I had known for some years, but now it broke with new revelation on my soul, and I found my confidence and conviction restored. It could be that not one human being was aware of my situation and praying (I was later to learn that the opposite was true—prayer, informed prayer, was ascending from God's servants in many nations on several continents), but one thing I knew: The Lord Jesus Christ, who spent 30 years in obscurity, then three-and-a-half years in dramatic public ministry, had for almost the last 2,000 years—to the exclusion of all other ministries—been engaged continuously in intercession. "For Christ is not entered into the holy places made with hands, which are the figures of the true; but into heaven itself, now to appear in the presence of God for us" (Hebrews 9:24, KJV). And He knew exactly what was happening. He cared and was able to deliver me.

Then a cold clamminess seemed to pervade the atmosphere, and I felt my throat muscles begin to tighten. I struggled to breathe. There could be no doubt as to the source of this intrusion. I began to recall the spiritual weapons God has given to His children in order to deal with situations like this one: the shield of faith, the sword of the Spirit, the blood of the Lamb, the Word of our testimony, the Name of the Lord Jesus Christ. In prayer, I used them all, but they brought only momentary relief. Then I felt God whisper, *Sing My praise. Declare My victory to the hosts of hell.*

I had never felt less able to sing. Into my mind flashed Psalm 27:1: "The LORD is my light and my salvation; whom shall I fear? the LORD is the strength of my life; of whom shall I be afraid?" (KJV). I squeaked rather than sang. Then I remembered Micah 7:8: "Rejoice not against me, O mine enemy: when I fall, I shall arise; when I sit in darkness, the LORD shall be a light unto me" (KJV).

By this time, my throat had loosened, and I was singing. The third Scripture I recalled was Psalm 68:1: "Let God arise, let his enemies be scattered" (KJV). I sang it through twice, rejoicing in the almightiness of my God. Whatever it was that had entered my room left just as quickly, and I was a wiser Christian. I had learned for the first time the effectiveness of the sung praises of God. I had entered into the experience of the psalmist in Psalm 149:6 (NASB): "Let the high praises of God be in their mouth, and a two-edged sword in their hand." It was not that the other weapons were less effective, but rather, that God was desiring to add another one to my armory.

Many times since that day, I have proved its mighty power. It is possible to sing our way to victory!

At four o'clock there was a knock on my door. I opened it. The interpreter greeted me politely and asked me to follow him. In the few short hours the day before, in which he had translated for me, I had come to appreciate him deeply and had prayed for wisdom and for an opportunity to share more adequately with him. Room 201 welcomed us again. It was the same group of men, with the exception of the official from ALBTURIST. He was not present at all the second day.

They inquired about my health and whether I had slept well. The chief then took up the attack again. With a smile, he said, "We knew all along that you were not from the Vatican. We know who you are. You are an intelligence agent, sent to spy on our land and our people." This was so ridiculous that I smiled as I declared that this was not true. The chief grew serious. He leaned across the table and, pointing his finger at me, he hissed, "I am a professional, and you are a professional, too!"

I remembered an incident that had occurred in the life of Corrie ten Boom, the wonderful Dutch saint, who was imprisoned by the Nazis for aiding Jews. She, too, was facing an interrogator. "Miss ten Boom," he said, "you must tell me everything. I may be able to do something, but only if you do not hide anything from me." It was then that Corrie realized that all his friendliness and his kindly concern were devices to elicit information. The man was a professional with a job to do. Corrie commented, "But I too, in a small way, was a professional."

During this second period of questioning, we covered almost the same ground as the day before. No doubt they were interested in whether I could give the same answers twice. The literature was again produced, and this time they read through "The Way of Salvation" booklet and commented among themselves concerning it. The chief then said to me, "Surely you don't believe the Bible. Why, it states that if someone smites you on the right cheek, you are to turn the other one to him also."

I smiled and said I did believe the Bible was the inspired Word of God and that when you understand and believe that love is the greatest power at work in the universe, that verse presents no problem. To this, the chief sneeringly replied—almost in the words of King Agrippa—"Are you trying to convert us?" I realized that I was not dealing with men who were ignorant of God nor of the teachings and claims of His Son, the Lord Jesus Christ. Interestingly, they never once threatened to destroy the Scripture booklets; rather, they took exceptional care, even to the extent of wrapping them in tissue paper. The burden to pray for the distribution of these booklets throughout the land is still on our hearts and on the hearts of those who pray for this nation. We firmly believe they are still in circulation.

Our tour group was scheduled to return in the early evening. I had left a note for Evey under her pillow, and I prayed that she might find it. I felt sure that she would be brought in for questioning also.

As the evening wore on, the men became impatient. The chief complained, "You refuse to cooperate with us. You refuse to tell the truth. We will imprison you for life." A chill went down my spine. Life imprisonment in the nation of Albania! More grace was going to be needed to accept this than to accept the death sentence.

For the last time they asked me the question, "Who sent you to Albania?" Again I replied that I was a Christian who loved and served God, that I had come at His command, and that I was prepared to bear full responsibility for my actions. I had known when I crossed the border the possible implications of what I was doing.

One of the interrogators then asked an interesting question: "Are there other people like you who are doing what you are doing?" Without realizing the impact of my reply, I said that yes, there were hundreds who were responding to the call of Jesus Christ to go to the uttermost parts of the earth—to the areas that have never heard, to difficult and dangerous lands behind the so-called Iron and Bamboo curtains; in short, to reach the entire world with the gospel of Jesus Christ.

Undisguised fear was written on his face as he asked a further question: "You mean others like you will come to Albania?" I told him that the command of the Lord Jesus was to go "into all the world"—and that included Albania.

Angrily, they led me out of Room 201. It was 11 o'clock. The interrogators lingered inside. While I waited in the corridor, the door of Room 202 opened. It was identical to Room 201. Behind a table sat several men. To the right sat Evelyn. She looked out as I looked in, and our eyes met in a long and meaningful embrace. We smiled. Many times in the course of the evening, she had asked both the Albanian guide and the interrogators, "Where is Miss Peterson?"

Their consistent reply was, "She is all right," but they would give no more information than that.

As a result of this moment, I believe I know what it must have been like to be in the crowd when the Jewish leaders gnashed their teeth in rage because of the simple presentation of truth by Stephen. "And he, full of the Holy Ghost, looked steadily into heaven and saw the glory of God." The imprint of divine glory must surely have been mirrored in Stephen's face.

When I looked at my friend Evey, there was a radiance about her that spoke of the beauty of the Lord Jesus. In the midst of heat and smoke, of blasphemy and anger, she sat serenely at peace with God and man. These men may well forget the faltering words we were able to speak, but will they ever be able to forget the visible demonstration of the reality of the life of the Lord Jesus? I believe Saul was never able to erase from his memory the moment when the life of Stephen was given so recklessly and therefore so powerfully to God. Did the beauty of that uplifted face haunt him until he, too, met Stephen's Lord on the Damascus road? To reach a nation for God, one must aim at its leaders, its government, its men of influence. How gracious of God to give us close to 20 hours with six of the key men in Enver Hoxha's Party!

My room looked the same as when I had left it, except for the addition of Evey's overnight bag. However, during this period when we were both being interrogated, the films were removed from our cameras and, most probably, a further search of our luggage was made. (In both of our suitcases was a film already exposed, and this was overlooked by them. We therefore left with these films intact and were able to develop them, once back in Switzerland.) I lifted Evey's pillow. There was the note undiscovered. I tore it into tiny pieces and dropped it into the wastebasket.

There was a gentle tap on the door. Outside stood the French guide. In a nervous whisper he asked, "What is wrong? What are they doing to you?" I pointed to my lips and then to the ceiling, and we scurried into the unoccupied room next door. He told me that when neither of us were at supper, he had become alarmed. One member of the group had seen Evey walking along the corridor with the Albanian guide, who appeared to be agitated and upset. The French guide told me that he had gone to the staff of the hotel and demanded to know what was happening, but nobody would tell him anything. He had decided to stay up all night if necessary and to maintain a watch outside our room in the hope that we would be returned. When he heard the footsteps of the interrogators bringing me back, he had hidden in the bathroom. Now he waited to hear all that I could tell him.

As simply as I could, I explained our reason for coming to Albania, that we were guilty of the act they had accused us of, and that we were prepared to accept the responsibility for our actions. I assured him that none of the other members of the group were implicated in any way. He did not rebuke or scold me. Instead, he identified closely as he shared the real reasons why he had come to Albania. Then he paused and said, "But to do a thing like this, your faith and belief in God must be very deep." It certainly was an unorthodox witnessing situation, but I welcomed the opportunity to share by both my life and my words the reality of the Lordship of Jesus Christ.

I told him that Evey was being interrogated in Room 202 and that her belongings were still in our room. We agreed together that it was most unlikely she would be returned to be with me again. Realizing this might be my only opportunity, I asked our guide to notify our friends in Switzerland of what had happened immediately upon his return to Paris, and he assured me he would do this. Then, in typical French fashion, he kissed me on both cheeks and said, "Vous etes brave, vous etes courageuse; je vais faire tout ce que je peux pour vous tier d'affaire." ("You are brave, you are courageous; I will do everything I can to rescue you.") With this we parted—he to maintain his vigil, and I to sleep. I lay for some time thinking about the events of the day.

Were these clever men bluffing? Would they dare to carry through either of their threats: death or life imprisonment? Could it be that, through laying down my life, a man the likes of Saul of Tarsus would come to know and serve Christ? Then my death would surely not be in vain. I could not expect the world to understand this; in human terms, it would appear such a waste of life and ability. But then I recalled the saying that in the 1950s had challenged a young American called Jim Elliot to go as a missionary and subsequently to lay down his life for the Auca Indians of Ecuador: "He is no fool who gives what he cannot keep to gain what he cannot lose."

Did I really believe that for the Christian the grave has no sting and death no victory? And what if it were to be life imprisonment? What were the jails of Albania like? Would there be anyone there who could speak English, or would I be forced to live in a world without communication? Would they allow me to work in the fields or the factories, or would I be classified as dangerous and confined to a solitary cell? Would they give me back my New Testament? How would they attempt to indoctrinate me? Would their methods be physical, as well as mental and emotional? Did I really believe that I could do all things through Christ who strengthens me—even to living out the remainder of my life in a prison in this hostile land?

What attempts would my family, friends, and country make to procure my release? Would they be able to bring sufficient pressure against such a militant government?

To what extent did this Communist nation value the increase of tourism and tourist money? Would this be a factor that would cause them to modify their punishment? Did they fear the effects of our particular tour group returning to the West with alarming tales of the arrest and retention of two members of the group?

If these men really believed that God did not exist, then why were they so afraid of the Word of God? Why did they classify it as "propaganda"? Why did they not immediately destroy the literature they recovered from our room? Why bring tissue paper to wrap it in? What did they intend to do with it?

In the midst of such thoughts, I fell asleep.

I woke with a start. Had I been dreaming? No, the room really was filled with people. I looked at my watch. It was 4:30 A.M. There was Evey with three or four men—presumably her interrogators—and her interpreter. She looked tired and a little pale, but she managed to smile at me. They commanded her to open her luggage and, as with me the night before, they went through all her belongings carefully. They demanded that she give up any remaining Scripture booklets. Faithfully, she endeavored to comply with their demand. When they later searched her handbag and found in a back pocket one more "Way of Salvation," they exploded with anger. It was useless for Evey to try to explain that this had not been deliberate but was a genuine oversight.

Their performance was almost identical to the night before. However, they had forgotten one thing: The previous night I was alone in the hotel, and their ranting and raving were for my benefit only. But now the tour group had returned, and many of the rooms on the floor were occupied. As I lay in bed, listening to the men question Evey, I became conscious of light footsteps in the corridor outside. I knew one set belonged to the French guide. But who else had been awakened and was listening to the performance with him?

This time, addressing us both, the interrogators announced, "You have one more opportunity to tell the truth before we are forced to imprison you. That will be in the morning!" They opened the door and were surprised to find a cluster of people outside. The French guide with real boldness demanded to know what was going on. We heard him say, "I have a right to know. I am responsible for them. I am their leader." He was firmly told that explanations would be given in the morning.

Mary was also in the group. Rather than talk in our room, I went back to her room with her and simply explained what had happened. She was afraid of being personally implicated because she had often been seen with us, and I had to comfort and assure her that this was not so. She had nothing to fear. Her roommate listened as I spoke. I knew that she was a committed young Communist, and I wondered what effect my words would have on her. Mary was visibly troubled as she said, "I am a Christian, but I knew better than to bring my Bible." She was convinced she would not be able to sleep a wink. Again, I attempted to reassure her that all was well.

Looking back now upon this incident, I believe it was a major reason for our release. The fact that several members of the group had witnessed this scene in the early hours of the morning meant that if we were detained, the story of what could happen to a tourist would begin to circulate. As in most Communist countries, tourist money is eagerly sought; adverse publicity could markedly reduce this.

Chapter Twelve

Father, Glorify Your Name

I returned from comforting Mary to find Evey stretched out on her bed. We hugged each other, then I knelt beside her, eager to hear all she had to share. She began first with details of her two-day journey into southern Albania.

With as much literature as possible stuffed into her brown leather handbag and into the large front pockets of her dress, Evey had boarded the bus for the journey into the heartland of Albania. The scenery rivaled anything that had been viewed previously. Quite without warning, a deep, narrow valley would give way to an expansive horizon of plains. Here, where only a few years ago small flocks of sheep and goats foraged among thornbushes and stunted shrubs, vineyards and fruit plantations now blossomed. Then from the plains the ascent began into high, forested mountains, only to change rapidly again as the bus descended to follow one of the most ancient arteries of communication—the road along which the feet of many invading and conquering armies had passed, as well as trade caravans headed for the East and West alike. It was here, along the Via Egnatia, that the Roman legions had marched on their route to conquest in the East.

This was the day we had prayed for when a visit would be made to the construction site of the railway being built by the "Young Volunteers." The impression had come strongly to us over the months that these young people were searching for truth—the truth that we had brought with us in booklet form.

Since 1970, the construction of the railway from Elbasan to the iron and nickel mines of Prenjas had been a matter of top priority for the Albanian government. Almost 14,000 volunteer young men and young women between 16 and 26 years of age—students, farmers, and workers—were accommodated in a huge camp at Elbasan. The camp consisted of five sections, each having 2,700 volunteers, and was further subdivided into six brigades of 450 persons. Work continued throughout the year, six days a week, and the daily schedule was rugged. Rising time was 4:30 A.M., and compulsory physical exercises preceded breakfast. At 5:30 A.M., marching in brigades with red flags at the head, the young people left the camp for work. A half-hour break was taken at 10:00, and construction work ended daily at 2:30 P.M. Lunch was served at 3:00, and siesta time lasted until 5:30. The evenings were devoted to sports and arts, organized at brigade level, and to political studies. For example, the report to the Sixth Congress by Enver Hoxha formed the basis of debate for several months between brigades. Plans initially called for this section of the railway, with its 21 tunnels and 300 bridges, to be completed by the beginning of 1974.

As in all Communist countries, the potential contribution of youth is not underestimated. A typical statement appearing in pamphlets given to tourists entering Albania reads as follows:

> It is a great asset to a people when its youth is unshaken, healthy, hard-working, full of zeal, and devoted to the cause of socialism. Tens of thousands of Albanian young people have taken part in national mass actions of building railroads and highways, in planting trees, in reclaiming new land, and in doing cultural work in the countryside. All these actions are schools for the revolutionary formation of the younger generation. Young farmers are required to spend two months each year at such actions, while students and workers spend one month. This prevents students from falling prey to intellectualism and gives them respect for physical labor. In the lives of the

> young farmers, it eliminates feudal, religious, and bourgeois complexes; but more importantly, it puts into their hands the ideological and political means to revolutionize their home areas when they return from the camp. When the freshness of youth unites with the proletarian ideology of Marxism-Leninism, it always feels in the spring of life.

In a land where 50 percent of the people are under 25 years old, provision is made for every age group. A feature of Albanian society is the Pioneer Camp for children aged 10 to 14 years. The biggest of these is at Camp Stefa at Durres, where 1,400 children can be accommodated. Again the camp is divided into three units of 450 children and further subdivided into 15 companies of 30 children. While at camp, the Pioneers do most of the work themselves—the preparation and cooking of meals, the care of the grounds, the organizing of the work schedule, etc. The purpose of these camps is the continuation of each child's education. Cultural and sports activities are organized. Swimming, poetry and singing, debates and discussions, and problem-solving sessions occur daily. As a result, it is confidently stated that Albania can count on its young people to defend Marxism-Leninism—the "invincible weapon of all people."

After passing through the city of Elbasan, the tour group reached the construction site of the railway. For many miles, they observed large groups of young people laboring at different tasks. Contrary to expectation, no stop was made to view the work. Only after considerable pressure had been applied by individual members on the Albanian guide was a 15-minute visit permitted.

Joyfully, Evey stepped out of the bus and was immediately surrounded by eager, curious young people. In limited French and English, they questioned her about world news and her own political convictions. Was she a Marxist-Leninist? "No," she firmly replied. This produced a noisy, although not "anti" reaction. If only she could give them the book that would explain the deep convictions of her life—but it was impossible. Why, then, had God given such expectation for this day and this visit in particular? It was hard to obey the order to return to the bus. Tomorrow they would return along the same route. Would an opportunity be given then? The possibility was remote.

Leaving the railway construction behind, it was announced that they were about to enter one of the great beauty spots of Albania—the area surrounding the Lake of Ohrid. This lake, which serves as the frontier with Yugoslavia, is large and exceptionally deep and clear. There was little traffic on the road, when suddenly two soldiers jumped in front of the bus. With guns pointed, they commanded the driver to stop. What could this mean? Evey felt the booklets in the pockets of her dress begin to burn holes in the fabric. After a heated exchange with the soldiers, the guide explained to the group that the house of an important Party member was a short distance up the road. Further access had been denied them, and the bus began to reverse.

The guide had second thoughts, however, and announced that another attempt would be made. The possibility that the soldiers would agree to the bus passing through—only after a thorough search of the passengers—was real, and Evey was anxious to transfer the literature from her pockets to her handbag. She requested a toilet stop—at which point the guide commented on how red her face was and asked her if she felt well. His kindness did nothing to quiet her pounding heart. She felt how awful it must be to live constantly with guilt feelings. At least, in this situation, she was guilty for the sake and cause of the Lord Jesus Christ! The toilet stop was arranged.

The second attempt to travel down the road was made. This time, after many words with the soldiers, permission was granted. When they reached the lake, it was hard to believe that the beautiful hills surrounding the basin of the lake were once stripped naked of their vegetation and left to the mercy of the forces of erosion. Today they were green with fruit and chestnut trees.

Toward early evening, the city of Korca—the principal city of southeastern Albania—was reached. There were few vehicles in evidence, but the streets were crowded with people, all on the move, arms linked, appearing to be going nowhere in particular. The wide main street was lined with lime trees, and their fragrance permeated the still, evening air.

The group stayed in a large, modern hotel, and Evey shared a room with a quiet, timid member of the group, Anne-Marie, a medical secretary in Paris. During the evening, she began to question Evey. What other lands had she visited? Afghanistan interested her in particular. Why had we been together in that land? What sort of work were we involved in? Evey shared as much as possible and promised more information on the plane journey home.

Before leaving her room in the morning, Evey placed a copy of "The Way of Salvation" on one of the higher shelves. How long would it be before a cleaning woman discovered it? Then a new idea came to her. If she placed a booklet in each clog, perhaps the opportunity would arise during the day to slip one out onto a factory floor or underneath a bush somewhere. Highlights of the morning were to be visits to two textile factories, one specializing in cotton materials and the other in rug and carpet-making. Considerable security measures were in force at both factories. The bus was not allowed to enter the factory proper; it had to park some distance away and the group was required to walk in.

The cleanness of the cotton factory was amazing. Hardly one piece of fluff could be found on the floor. This was no place to be sliding booklets out of one's shoe onto the floor! Also, uniform plastic sandals are worn by almost every adult and child. Foreign footwear is therefore conspicuous. This was true in the factory. Evey discovered that the workers would look often at her feet before her face!

Almost by chance, she met a midwife in the factory, and they began to share a little. She assured Evey that the women were taken good care of and were able to keep medical appointments during their working hours. A visit to the toilet before leaving the factory gave Evey the chance to place one more Gospel of John.

While walking to the second textile factory, Evey felt a little like the Pied Piper of Hamlin—children began to come alongside and follow her. Out came the faithful phrase book, and, simply, she began to ask, "What is your name?" "How old are you?" "What school do you go to?" They were delighted to reply. The word love was also in the phrase book. With care, Evey told them that "Jesus is love." There was little reaction. During this walk, an adult would occasionally come up and remove a child from the group and hustle him or her away. An older brother also clouted his little brother and dragged him off, but in no way was it a repeat of the scene that had greeted us our first day in the land in the city of Shkodra.

Evey sensed it was important to be alone and not walking with other group members, wherever possible. As she stood on a street corner, an elderly woman with hands gnarled from hard labor approached her. Looking into Evey's face, she began to speak in

Albanian. With a silent prayer to God, Evey replied. The woman responded, and Evey spoke again. The woman spoke a third time.

At this moment, the French guide appeared and asked her to rejoin the group. It was time to visit the second factory. Almost all the workers in this particular rug and carpet factory were women—a surprising occurrence when it is remembered that the factory operates 24 hours a day. Again, the place was scrupulously clean. All the wool was fed into the machines by hand, and it appeared that four women were working on each rug or carpet.

The return to Durres was uneventful until just north of Pogradec when the railway line came into view again. Heavy rains had fallen through the night, badly affecting the surface of the road. Two trucks were stopped up ahead, and in front of them was a large vehicle, obviously bogged down in the mud and blocking the road in both directions. There was no alternative but to stop the bus. As soon as permission was granted, Evey was out of the bus. This was the reason for the literature in her clog. Deftly, she slipped it under a bush on the side of the road. Once the vehicles moved on, it would be easily recovered by one of the "Young Volunteers."

Within minutes, the strength of the volunteers had been applied to the stuck truck, and the traffic flowed again. Few of the group had even bothered to leave the bus. The One who specializes in impossibilities had done it again!

The group returned to Durres in the early evening, a little ahead of schedule. Evey raced up the stairs, eager to find out how I was. Her first impression, as she entered the room, was how tidy everything was. I must surely be recovered. Perhaps I was down at the beach or having supper in the dining room. She set out to find me. Walking toward her along the corridor was the Albanian guide. He looked distressed as he said, "You must come with me."

A beautiful thing had occurred during the two-day trip. As our group numbered 20, we were paired off on the bus. Evey and I normally sat together. Now she had been alone. So, too, was the Albanian guide. Thus, Evey had invited him to sit with her. There was so much to talk about and so much to learn from him concerning the land and the people. Unlike so many other members of the group, who were frustrated and angry about the many cancellations and changed schedules, Evey was happy to be in the land and genuinely interested in learning all she could about the country—grateful for his assistance and concern for the welfare of the whole group.

The Albanian guide was obviously impressed. Before the trip was completed, he changed from using the French "you," meaning a person in general, to a much more intimate "you," meaning a member of the family or a close friend. Certain members of the group picked this up and questioned Evey about it. She could only reply that he must be regarding her as a friend. It was therefore painful for him to be sent to arrest her.

As they walked along the corridor, he exclaimed, "But I cannot understand it! You are an educated person! You are a scientist! How can you believe in God?"

Evey replied, "That is not difficult for me. Every time I help to bring a new life into this world (Evey is a midwife), I am a witness to a miracle of God. I cannot but believe in Him."

Firmly entrenched in the minds of the interrogators was the belief that I had forced Evey—indeed, paid her!—to accompany me on this mission. She was only an accomplice. Because of this, through the eight long hours of questioning, Evey was presented with a significant opportunity to give her own personal testimony of the detailed leading and guidance of God. She affirmed her willingness to bear responsibility for her actions. Her simple, direct answers unnerved them. When they resorted to blasphemy and vulgarity, Evey spoke to her interpreter and told him that she found their blasphemy offensive and would he ask the interrogators to cease using this sort of language. Nervously, the interpreter conveyed her request. They responded in anger. Evey believed they continued to use the same language, but the interpreter did not translate it.

This incident occurred after I had been returned to my room, and Evey was using my interpreter—the young man whom I had grown to appreciate so much.

At one point, they produced an impressive collection of papers. Then they said to Evey, "You are not nearly as clever as Miss Peterson. She has told us everything; this is all the evidence she has given us." Then, producing two or three pieces of paper, they said, "This is all you have told us."

Evey replied, "I'm not clever, but I am honest." We have laughed many times at the possible interpretation of her answer: Miss Peterson is clever, but Miss Muggleton is honest? For almost every question that was asked, Evey managed to bring God into the answer. Exasperated at last, they thundered, "Don't mention the name of God again!" They phrased their next question to her, "Who sent you to Albania?"

Evey replied, "I am sorry, gentlemen. I know you have asked me not to mention the name of God again, but if I am to answer your question truthfully, I have to say, 'God sent me.'"

It was already daylight, but we had so much to share with each other. We discovered we had been asked the same questions, but, alas, to many key ones we had given different answers! We had both spoken the truth, but this would be difficult to explain to the officials. For example, they asked me what my occupation was, and I said I was a secretary. They asked Evey what I did, and she said I was a teacher. Both answers were true. They asked me where I met Evey, and I said I had met her in Ethiopia. They asked Evey where she had met me, and she responded in England en route to Afghanistan. We had met in both these places. They asked me where I had obtained the literature, and I said it had come to me from Holland and Germany. They asked Evey where it had come from, and she said from England. (Because the literature was printed in England, Evey presumed that was where I had obtained it.) We were deeply aware that we were in an impossible situation.

In all their searching, they had not discovered Evey's diary. In it was a detailed account of where we had left the literature. This had to be destroyed. It would be unwise simply to tear it into small pieces and throw it in the wastebasket. I had bought a box of Albanian matches for a friend who collects matchboxes. Gratefully, I began to burn the incriminating pieces of paper. Now there was a charred mass in the washbasin. I turned on the tap—alas, no water! Then I remembered it was turned off at night. How unprofessional we were at such things! We trusted that we would be undisturbed until the water was turned on in the morning. The smell of smoke was strong. We opened the windows wide and sprayed perfume in the air.

We prayed before attempting to sleep. We told the Lord we recognized that without His help we were in a hopeless position. We confessed that we did not feel very brave or heroic. We asked Him, through our weakness, to manifest His strength. We thanked Him for the grace that He had already given, for the peace that reigned in our hearts—even as the interrogators sustained their threat to imprison us. We told Him our eyes were upon Him and that we trusted Him for all that the third day of interrogation would bring.

The steady, regular breathing from the adjoining bed told me that Evey was already asleep. I closed my eyes and remembered, "In the time of trouble he shall hide me in his pavilion....He shall set me up upon a rock. And now shall mine head be lifted up above my enemies" (Psalm 27:5-6, KJV).

The noise of people walking in the corridor outside our room woke me. My first thoughts were of the ashes in the washbasin. I turned on the tap and removed every trace of the burned paper. Should I join the rest of the group for breakfast? No one had said I couldn't. Evey was still sleeping. I entered the dining room, and the French guide motioned to me to join him. Several of the group noted my entry, but no one joined us at the table. I was still without an appetite, but I enjoyed the good, strong coffee. Giving an outward appearance of being ultracasual, I brought him up to date. Between mouthfuls of scrambled eggs, he told me of his intentions to bring every possible pressure to bear to secure our release. I told him how grateful I was for his attitude and concern.

The group was to leave at nine for a day's excursion down the southwestern coast to visit the much-talked-about Mao Tse-tung textile factory at Berat and the Roman ruins at Appollonia close by the city of Fier.

When I returned to the room, Evey was awake. We agreed that whatever the day held, it would not be dull—that was certain! We recalled a New Year's Eve message given by Don Stephens, the European director of Youth With A Mission. He had spoken from 2 Kings, chapter 2, concerning the hard thing that Elisha asked of Elijah. He challenged us to ask of God a hard thing for the New Year of '73—something that was far bigger than we were. Evey and I had both done this, and it had set the tone for our year. Now we were in a very hard place facing a very hard situation!

There was faith in our hearts to ask God for deliverance. We could recall many Bible verses in which God had promised this very thing. Verses like Psalm 50:15 (KJV): "Call upon me in the day of trouble: I will deliver thee and thou shalt glorify Me." Why was God not giving us the liberty to pray this way? We waited in silence before Him, and He spoke the same thing into both our hearts: *It is your right, as My children, to ask for deliverance. My Son was in a similar situation. His soul was troubled and He said, "What shall I say? Father, save me from this hour: but for this cause came I unto this hour. Father, glorify thy name"* (John 12:27-28, KJV).

God was asking us whether we trusted Him enough to leave the situation in His hands. Were we really concerned with His glory? Could we truly say, "Father, glorify Your Name. You know whether You can best do this by our death, by our imprisonment, or by our release. We leave that decision with You"? The prayer of relinquishment was what God was longing to hear from our lips. His grace was made available. We each prayed out loud, using the other as a witness, and we relinquished our lives to Him.

A knock at the door occurred simultaneously with the end of the second prayer. Our French guide stood outside and said he had been sent to fetch us. A meeting was to take place with the other members of the tour group in a downstairs lounge.

CHAPTER THIRTEEN

No Weapon That Is Formed Against You Shall Prosper

As we walked along the corridor with our guide, other members of the group came out of their rooms and walked in the same direction. Our worst fears were realized—the group was being punished for our crime! It was now 11 o'clock, and they should have departed two hours ago. Our destination was a large room on the ground floor. At the head of the room was a long table, behind which sat several of our interrogators, our Albanian guide, the minister from ALBTURIST, and a new face: the chief prosecutor of the land.

The group assembled, a curious mixture of expressions on their faces. Some looked fearful and apprehensive, others mystified, not a few impatient. One relaxed member (apparently oblivious of the night's proceedings) laughed as he said in a loud voice, "What's this? An interrogation or something?" The chairs were spread in a semicircle facing the table, and Evey and I sat with the French guide a little to the left of center.

Conversation ceased, and the prosecutor rose to speak. The Albanian guide interpreted. At length, and with considerable dramatic effect, the official began his speech. He expressed his sorrow to the group for their detention, and then went on to explain that, unknown to the Albanian government, two members of this particular tour group were criminals who had crept across the border undetected. Once in the country they had committed crimes against the glorious People's Republic of Albania. The eyes of the group turned toward us. Many expressed shock and amazement.

After a moment, the prosecutor spoke again: "Will the two criminals please stand."

We stood. This must surely be an effort at public humiliation. Then came the declaration of our crime. We had smuggled religious propaganda into the land—portions of the Bible in the Albanian language—and distributed it throughout the country. There was an almost audible expression of relief from the more tense group members, ardent Socialists though most of them were.

The prosecutor continued. "We have seriously considered how to punish these criminals. They are guilty and therefore worthy of imprisonment. However, because they are young girls (this was quite flattering), we have decided to release them. We will drive them to the border and leave them there, declaring them to be *personae non grata*" (i.e., not able to enter Albania again). Evey had been faithfully interpreting the prosecutor's speech into English for me. But my ears were not prepared to hear this! Had she interpreted it correctly? Were we to be released? Could it be possible?

I was still trying to take this in when one of the group got to his feet and said in quite angry fashion, "I demand to know what is wrong with bringing Christian literature into the country!" This was unbelievable! I was thinking how marvelous it was that such a challenge should be given, but Evey was concerned lest they think that others were involved in our crime.

A real hubbub broke out, with considerable interchange in Albanian and French. I believe that for many it was an opportunity to vent some suppressed frustrations and anger. Members of the group began to come over to us, especially the women, and express their love and concern. Some inquired whether we had sufficient money to get home. Others wrote out their names and addresses in France and handed them to us. One woman even remarked, "You have done this because your faith in God is real."

Without warning, I felt the tears begin to flow. At no other time had I come remotely close to weeping, and to be honest, now I was a little embarrassed by it. Our chief interrogator saw it and seized the opportunity to say, "If you had thought more carefully about your actions, you would not have to be crying now." How could he be expected to understand that these were tears of joy and gratitude to God for His love and grace—not the tears of self-pity and remorse that he suspected?

A further announcement was made. The group would depart immediately on their tour, and we two would go to our room and pack our suitcases. The police vehicle was waiting outside the hotel to take us to the border. The authorities had intended this episode to dishonor our credibility and defame the name of Christ. Instead, God had presented us with an unparalleled opportunity to share with our entire group our reasons for being in the land. When death to self has taken place, public humiliation is not difficult to bear. Identification with the Savior, who in His humiliation was denied even justice, was a very real privilege.

We bounded up the steps, two at a time. When safe in our room, we hugged each other and danced and sang. Within minutes we had packed our belongings, but what would we do with our Albanian leks? The only things for sale at the hotel were postcards, so while I set off to purchase some, Evey wrote a short note to our friend Hélène. She was Mary's roommate, the brilliant young student from Paris. She was with us the night we went into Durres. Because she was fluent in English, we had enjoyed her company on the bus, at mealtimes, and on other occasions. We had learned that she was a student of economics and languages and, although only 17, she had already completed her first year of university study. When questioned about her philosophy of life, she had shared that she was committed to Marxist-Leninist principles and that she had been able to spend time as an exchange student in Russia. She spoke Russian fluently, as well as French and English. We had noticed that she had limited pocket money. Therefore, Evey put some leks in an envelope with a short note, urging her to buy a souvenir with it. Evey also gave her our home address. It was a simple matter to slip the envelope under the door of her room.

As I walked toward the lobby where the postcards were displayed, I was surprised to find the chief interrogator and the interpreter walking toward me. With an undisguised sneer, the chief said, "So you thought you were free! There are more questions we require you to answer. It depends on how you answer these further questions whether we will release you or not." They commanded me to return with them to Room 201. The moments that followed were exceedingly difficult. The announcement of our release had resulted in a total relaxation—of mind, heart, body, and spirit. I was to be freed!

Must I now enter into combat again? Had the announcement so dramatically given to our tour group been just a fabrication of lies? Had they been fooled into believing we would be released? Now they had departed. The authorities were free to do with us as they liked, and no one would be the wiser. The thought was chilling!

The chief's opening remarks were, "Your mission is an absolute failure. But you are a professional, and we cannot afford to let professionals go so easily. We will wait for Miss Muggleton to join us. Then we will proceed with further questioning."

Within a few minutes Evey arrived. We looked at each other without smiling. They spoke first to Evey. "Are you responsible for your actions?"

"Yes," replied Evey, "I have told you many times that I accept this responsibility."

The interrogators continued. "But Miss Peterson shall keep responsibility."

Evey looked at me and was sharply commanded to look only at the interrogators. We were told we were to have no communication whatsoever between ourselves. She replied, "No, we each accept responsibility for our actions."

They said firmly, "No, Miss Peterson shall keep responsibility."

Did the interpreter find it difficult to translate clearly into English, or were they saying what we thought they were saying? One of us was more guilty than the other. It was not possible to share responsibility. They would consider acquitting one, provided the other could be declared guilty. They then began to repeat the questions they had asked us so many times before—to which, if pressed to an ultimate point, we would have to reply, "I am not able to give you that answer." Questions like: Who had sent the literature to us? How did we happen to both be in countries so far apart as Ethiopia and Afghanistan? What school did I teach at?

It was at this time that we witnessed a marvelous thing take place. As they phrased their questions, we knew what they were leading up to. Yet, as they would approach a critical point (after laying a careful foundation), they would immediately—without any explanation—veer away and begin to ask a completely new set of questions. This happened not once, but every time they came close to a question to which we were not willing to give them an answer. We recalled Loren Cunningham's prayer: "May there be a release of God in the land."

I believe these intelligent, highly skilled men must even today recall with pain, embarrassment and wonder their endeavors to solicit the truth. So many times they reminded us of deflated balloons as, filled with self-importance and arrogant confidence, they hurled their questions at us, only to crumple and deflate as the wisdom of God left them without reply.

The scribe then produced a huge bundle of papers. This was all the written evidence that had accumulated during the interrogation. Each page had to be translated for us, and we were then instructed to sign it. Evey and I had identical pages. This took a considerable amount of time and put a real strain on the interpreter.

Then, in contrast to the mass of papers that were written by hand, an official-looking typed sheet was produced. The chief addressed me and said that this was a list of the crimes I had committed against the People's Republic of Albania. Evey did not have one of these sheets. I was asked for my signature, so I requested that it be translated. Strangely, they refused this. I replied that I could only sign it when it had been translated. Again they refused. Were we about to have an ugly confrontation? I felt Evey stiffen at my side. I sent up an arrow prayer: "God, if I sign this, I could be signing my death warrant." The answer from heaven was swift and direct: *Sign it and trust Me.* Another arrow prayer: "But, Father...." And another swift reply: *Remember, your times are in My hands. You are not at the mercy of these interrogators.* So I signed the statement.

The interrogators left the room, and the scribe asked, rather apologetically, if he could go over some of the evidence to make sure his English was correct. Did we imagine it, or did he purposely single out the paragraphs that contained our Christian testimony as the ones he needed to have us explain more fully? For several minutes we answered his questions. How we did appreciate the help he had given us, and we were grateful for the opportunity to express this to him!

A hotel worker appeared, and the interpreter explained that a meal had been served for us in the dining room. This really surprised us. It was now two o'clock on Wednesday afternoon. My last meal had been Sunday supper. I could not explain my lack of hunger nor my adequate physical strength, but with the announcement of the meal, my appetite returned. We sat alone in the very large dining room, being served a three-course dinner.

We were still uncertain of what they really intended to do with us. It was very possible that they planned to separate us, perhaps to release Evey and detain me. But we were learning to recognize and appreciate God's intervention in the present and to trust Him with the future. Our meal completed, we returned to our room, collected our belongings, and then made our way to the police car parked at the entrance of the hotel. It was not quite what we had expected. A driver was laboring with a crank handle to start an ancient Volvo.

We still had a considerable amount of Albanian money which would be worthless to us should we be released from the country. When our interpreter appeared, we told him this and asked him if we could change it. Our minds said, "Of course not; it's useless even to ask such a thing!" When the vehicle finally coughed and spluttered into action, however, we drove first to the Adriatica Hotel, and in a matter of minutes our Albanian leks were returned to us in the form of French francs. This was the first real indication that maybe they did intend to release us. But would we both taste freedom—or would the joyous release of one be tempered by the retention of the other?

The police car was very obviously a four-passenger vehicle. Yet six crowded into it. The chief interrogator, Evey, myself, and the scribe sat in the backseat—in that order. The driver and interpreter took the front seats. Why did we have such an important escort? We knew that for the first few kilometers the road that led to the northern border also led to the capital, Tirana. For which were we bound? That was the all-important question! Our first stop after the Adriatica was a petrol pump, and then we began the journey.

Prayer was more important to us than conversation. While our escorts talked among themselves, we again took our place of authority over all the devices and strategies of the evil one. There was no doubt in our minds that a battle was being waged at this very moment in the heavenlies. What joy to know that "far greater is Jesus Christ in us than all the combined power of the principalities of darkness." We renewed again our relinquishment of the right to be delivered if God could be more greatly glorified by our imprisonment or death.

I had often wondered what it would be like to be in a difficult or dangerous situation and unable to pray aloud. Was silent prayer just as effective? Now I had the answer to my question. Our four Albanian friends were oblivious to the fact that prayer was being made to God—that defeats were being handed out to the hosts of wickedness in heavenly places. Evey and I were conscious of not only spiritual victories taking place but, as we prayed, encouragement, strength, and peace flooded our own souls.

We had driven for about 30 minutes when the chief interrogator thumped the driver on the back, and the car screeched to a halt. A large truck had stopped in front of us, and workmen, with an assortment of shovels, spades, and pickaxes in their hands, were jumping off. Their work for the day must have ended, but why were they being left here? Would they walk the rest of the way to their houses? This appeared to be a road junction of some importance.

Then, both back doors of our car opened, and the chief and the scribe got out. They gave us a brief nod and then slammed the doors shut. The driver started the engine, and we took a sharp turn to the left, entering an empty road. No explanation was given to us, and we did not dare to ask for one.

Could it mean that we were now on the road that would take us to the border? Had we left the scribe and the interrogator on the road that went to Tirana? Would they hitch a lift to the city? Was it possible that we were *both* going to be released? Once earlier in the day, we had relaxed prematurely. We would not make the same mistake twice. Was this indeed the road to Shkodra that we had traveled by night on our first evening in Albania? Everything was unfamiliar; we had no way of knowing where we were or where we were going. Could there be a prison for criminals who smuggled propaganda into the land somewhere in the northern regions of the nation?

After about an hour, the interpreter spoke sharply to the driver, and we stopped suddenly. On the other side of the road, several vehicles were parked—mainly trucks. Behind a high hedge was a tea garden of sorts. Roughly hewn tables were attached to wobbly legs. Long planks served for benches. So many feet had trampled the ground that the grass long ago had been reduced to bare earth. The interpreter ordered four cups of tea, and we drank gratefully. The place was hot and dusty, and the police car emitted powerful fumes which had served to dry our mouths and throats. As we sipped our tea, we became objects of curiosity—two foreigners traveling in a police car with a two-man escort! That was not a normal everyday occurrence!

We drove on. Two men jumped onto the road and commanded us to stop. The pig disease again! We left the vehicle while it labored through the strip of straw. Then it was our turn to walk through it. In my enthusiasm, I stomped too heavily and immediately plunged up to my ankles in foul-smelling disinfectant. My distress was immediately recognized. A roadside worker came with a bucket of water and poured it over my foot and then over my clog, and he and I laughed together about it. In spite of his efforts, however, my clog now bore a permanent memory of Albania etched on its suede!

We resumed our journey, approaching a populated area. Was this the city of Shkodra? It looked as if it could be. Yes, it was—there was the austere and crumbling Fortress of Rozefat dominating the city. So we were traveling directly north. The border of Hani Hotit could only be, at the most, an hour's drive away. Then an unhappy thought came to me: Would the same guards be on duty at the border as the day we had entered? If so, could we expect an ugly scene with the men who had searched our luggage? We had lived through so much in the past three days, and God had been so faithful and His strength so sufficient that if this was necessary before those massive, barbed-wire gates swung open and we were escorted into no-man's-land, we would survive!

The scenery was now familiar: the squalid little villages surrounded by fields of corn and wheat, the rustic stone bridges that allowed the mountain streams to flow on undisturbed to the sea.

The presence of groups of soldiers became more and more noticeable. The interpreter spoke with the driver. We stopped at the entrance to a military camp. Was this the one we had passed on our way into the land? Were we less than a mile from the border? The interpreter left the car and walked up the long driveway to the barracks, having first shown his pass. The driver turned on a radio and treated us to the Albanian equivalent of "Top of the Pops"—or maybe we were close enough to Yugoslavia to be picking up one of their stations.

We waited for 20 minutes. The interpreter returned without comment, and we drove on.

Within minutes, the familiar border buildings were in view. We had never expected to see them again. The area appeared to be absolutely deserted. There were no vehicles coming or going, no men to be seen. On the side of a nearby mountain, spelled out with huge stones that had been painted white, was the slogan that had greeted us upon our arrival: "Parti Enver". It had been almost meaningless to us when we first read it, but in the course of seven days, we had come to understand something of the power and influence upon the nation of this man who has ruled with an iron fist for over 30 years. During the tour, Mary had explained that this sign was placed at the border for the special purpose of aggravating the Yugoslavians.

It was six in the evening. Politely, the interpreter asked for our passports. We handed them to him.

We had no desire to enter the buildings or to make contact with the border officials. Alas, the drama of the day and the long journey made it necessary for us to find a bathroom. Trying to look as inconspicuous as possible, we entered through a side door. We endeavored to explain our need to a cleaning lady, and she understood and pointed out the place. Sadly, no cleaning had been done there in a long time! We returned to the car. How long a short period of time can appear!

How large would the *personae non grata* be in our passports? Would it take up a whole page? The entry stamp had been most unimpressive—just a small triangle with the date, the name of the border, and up one side of the triangle the word *Shquiperi.* (This is the name used by Albanians to refer to their country.) The interpreter left the Customs building and came toward the car, our two passports in his hand. Gravely, he handed them to us. This was not the moment to look inside. He opened the trunk and lifted our two cases out. He handed them to us, and with no emotion in his voice, he said, "You may go." We picked up our cases and walked through the gates into no-man's-land. We did not pause to look back. We heard the gates close behind us. Was our mission a failure?

No! He, the King of glory, would cause these ancient gates to open again! Perhaps not to us, but to others like us who would hear and respond gladly to His commission to go into all the world, particularly to the lands where Christ is not named. As it is written, "To whom he was not spoken of, they shall see: and they that have not heard shall understand" (Romans 15:21, KJV).

Chapter Fourteen

For My Angel Will Go Ahead of You

We viewed no-man's-land with new eyes. No longer did it appear just an endless succession of swamps. We breathed deeply, we laughed, we sang. We put down our suitcases and sat by the side of the road and thanked God for His deliverance. We told Him how sweet freedom tasted. We opened our passports. There by the entry stamp was a conventional exit stamp—the same as the tour group would receive when they flew out of Tirana the following day! The only difference would be ours was dated a day earlier. How could this be? There was no natural explanation!

Back at the border, now about half a mile away, a truck was pulling out, bound for Germany—or was it France? We stood up and waved, but the driver did not look at us as he drove past. We recalled our first efforts at hitchhiking two weeks earlier on the Geneva motorway. At least we were not amateurs! But what sort of vehicle could we expect to meet in this forsaken part of the world? The thought didn't trouble us. The fact that ahead of us stretched 1000 kilometers of Yugoslavian coastline, and then the entire section of northern Italy, was of little concern. We could truly say with the apostle Paul, "None of these things move me." Time would be needed to crystallize the significance of the experiences we had lived through. Our minds refused even to dwell upon them. The God who had delivered us by His mighty power—how would He bring us home to Switzerland?

We picked up our cases and walked on. The thought of sleeping out under the stars appealed to us enormously, for the Yugoslavian border, we felt, was still some ten kilometers away. The sound of an engine, however, soon caught our attention. It was too gentle to be that of an Albanian truck. A baby Fiat came to a stop beside us.

A young man got out and said, "Taxi?" With surprise, we answered, "Yes," but held out our empty hands and said, "No diner" (Yugoslavian currency). He stood for a while looking at us, then shook his head, got into his car, and drove back the way we had come. We felt a little like both laughing and crying. The laughable part was a taxi appearing in the middle of nowhere. Where had he come from, and where was he returning to? It was a mystery. The crying part was that our cases became heavier the longer we carried them, and it surely would have been nice to be driven to the next border.

We were just discussing whether we could afford to throw our cases away and so appear like normal hitchhikers when we heard the sound of an engine again. Back it came—the same car driven by the same young man. This time he simply got out, put our cases in the trunk, opened the door, and motioned for us to get in. We obeyed without asking questions. He drove us to the border, handed us our luggage, smiled, and drove back the same way he had come.

There was no time to think further about who he was, where he had come from, why he had not taken us the first time, but then returned again a second time, for a guard was coming toward us out of the small Customs building. He seemed to understand the situation immediately. We were ushered into his office and given royal treatment. Only later did we learn that anyone who is thrown out of Albania automatically becomes a hero in Yugoslavian eyes. Although limited by language, the men at the border expressed real hospitality, and peaches and chocolate became our evening meal.

When we mentioned our need to reach Titograd, a southern city in Yugoslavia about 35 kilometers away, there were immediate protests. Surely we would accept their invitation and stay the night with them there at the border! We remained gently adamant, and when they realized we could not be persuaded otherwise, an official offered to drive us to Titograd if we would pay for the petrol. We gladly agreed to this and worked out a reasonable equivalent in French francs. Knowing Titograd well, they drove us to an ideal camping site in the city. A tent was available, and we wasted no time in putting our valuables under a pillow and sleeping for the night.

As in most summer campgrounds, the day began really early. Tempted though we were to rest for a day, we got out our map and began to work out the route we should take. The story of the map is an interesting one. We were unsure, when in Switzerland, whether the tour group would provide us with any information or with a map of Albania, so Evey tried to buy one before leaving. It was impossible. Every shopkeeper said the same thing: "We are never asked for a map of that country." In one shop, however, Evey studied a map of Yugoslavia and found that it included Albania. She gladly bought it. Now we were faced with making our own way up the entire length of Yugoslavia—a journey neither of us had made before. Without the map, it would have been impossible.

Since the early 1970s, the coast of Yugoslavia has become one of the most popular holiday resorts in the whole of Europe, perhaps unrivaled on the Continent for natural beauty. It is one of the few countries that has not sold out to the cotton-candy and cola cult. Its palm-shaded bistros and island-dotted coastline are not lost in neon and plastic. Historic towns and sleepy mountain villages still echo the flavor of hundreds of years of Greek, Roman, Turkish, and Venetian influence.

As we pored over the map, we realized we were about to have two vacations instead of one. But first we had to make our way out of Titograd. That proved to be difficult, and we learned our first lesson in the art of hitchhiking: avoid cities wherever possible. The sun was hot, even though it was still early morning, and traffic was sparse. There were two horse- or donkey-drawn carts to every four-wheeled vehicle. A series of short lifts brought us to Budva by midday. What beauty! Here in the south, it was still relatively unspoiled. We rested a while and began to note the different registrations on the cars. This country must be where East meets West. During the short time that we sat on a wall quenching our thirst with a bottle of Coke, we counted ten nations, four of them Eastern European.

A friendly lady stopped and smiled at us. She spoke a little

German, but said that she was Russian. How we wished we had more to give her than our smiles! We got back on the road just as the heavens opened and a torrential downpour brought welcome relief to the parched earth. We welcomed it also because it served to bring us an instant ride. We did much better in the afternoon, even getting picked up by a bus and, without charge, being taken a little beyond the city of Dubrovnik. Then came our best lift of the day. A kind man with two children stopped for us. He was traveling to the big city of Split, and we drove with him for several hours. Having mastered our first lesson, we asked him to let us off a few kilometers before the city. This he did, and in a little town called Omis, we found a local house that had a sign outside it saying "Chambres, Zimmer." A motherly woman answered the door and showed us her guest room. It was clean and totally adequate. Our few words of German were sorely tested as we explained it was for one night and we would have breakfast in the morning. Her garden fronted the beach, so we decided to take a stroll before sleeping. Music coming from a beach café tempted us to enter.

Once inside, the cucumbers and tomatoes looked so good that we just had to sample them. We returned to our house, and there waiting for us was a meal of steak and tomatoes and cucumbers. Our German was obviously more limited than we imagined; instead of breakfast, we had asked for supper!

We agreed that an early-morning swim would be refreshing. Although at six A.M. the water temperature could hardly be described as warm, it was bracing and a good way to start the day. We were on the road by seven. Whether our superior progress on the second day was the result of an increased flow of traffic or because we were becoming more skilled remains debatable, but our first lift was a good one. From Titograd to Split, we had sampled 14 different vehicles. On our second day, we were to have only five and yet cover twice as much ground. The northern city of Rijeka proved to be a problem. We reached it at four in the afternoon. After many inquiries, we then caught a bus to the outer town limits and began to hitch again.

This was our worst experience. There were many vehicles of all sorts, but no one appeared to have time to stop. We had developed a good system. I would stay somewhat in the background, trying to minimize the size of our two embarrassingly large suitcases, while Evey would use the time-honored signal of thumbing. If a driver responded, she would quickly put her head in the window and, using the map, would point to the route we were taking. If the driver was agreeable, she would call me, and we would gratefully climb in.

We had stood for what seemed a very long time when an ultra-smart vehicle came to a stop. The driver was going in our direction and was willing to take us. Within minutes, we were on our way, traveling with the director of an opera company. His coiffure was finely guarded in a net, and his conductor's dress suit hung in the back of the car. He was rushing through from his holiday home in Rijeka for an evening performance in Ljubljana. Stimulating conversation flowed back and forth, and we regretted when our destinations caused us to separate. The next vehicle that stopped was a petrol tanker. Beggars cannot be choosers, so we climbed into the cab. The view of the countryside from such a high elevation was excellent. Unfortunately, he was not crossing into Italy. We were deposited in the center of a small village, just a few kilometers from the border.

It was now seven o'clock, and we stood debating what we should do. Was it wise to attempt to go any further...to hitchhike across Italy at night? Maybe we could accept one more ride before it became dark and then find a place to stay. How, though, would we overcome the problem of not having any Italian money? While we talked, a car stopped. Evey showed the driver the direction we wanted to go and he nodded, so we climbed into the backseat. Realizing we were almost at the border, we put both our passports on the unoccupied front seat.

We recognized our arrival at the border by the long line of cars stopped ahead of us. Inspection was going to take a considerable amount of time. To our surprise, our driver pulled out of the normal lane and began to accelerate in a lane all by himself. When we came to the Passport Control, he did not even attempt to pick up our passports off the seat; he simply made a movement with his hand to the officer and drove straight through. This was our first experience of leaving a Communist border in *such* fashion! Surely we must be traveling with a high-ranking Yugoslav official!

We were now at the Italian border. Again, there was a long line of cars patiently waiting to be processed, and again our driver pulled out of the normal lane and accelerated into a lane by himself. This time as he approached the control point, he made no sign whatsoever, but just drove straight through and on into Italy! We looked at each other in amazement. Who were we driving with? There could be a natural explanation for crossing one border this way, but two borders—never! After about ten kilometers, we came to a small Italian village. He pulled up at a bus stop and we got out. He also got out. He reached into his pocket and, putting a large number of silver coins into my hand, he looked at me firmly and explained, "Bus, Trieste; Trieste, Train." He then returned to his car and drove off.

Within a few minutes a bus arrived and we boraded it. I put all the silver coins down beside the driver and said, "Trieste." He counted them slowly and gave us two tickets and no change. Within 20 minutes, the lights of Trieste were clearly visible. The driver let us off only a block away from the train station.

Though we had discussed it several times, we had not made a decision as to how to cross Italy, but we remembered the stranger's injunction. We inquired about a train to Milan and found that one left in 30 minutes. We had just enough time to change French francs into Italian lira, purchase the tickets, buy some food, find the platform, and climb aboard. It was a crowded train. We found two seats, though, and made ourselves comfortable for the night. The low fare of the Italian trains amazed us. It seemed we might even have enough money left to be able to train-ride right through to Lausanne!

After having stopped countless times through the night, we reached Milan in the early morning. There was a train leaving for Lausanne within the hour. We raced to the bank. Alas, it was still closed and would not open for another two hours! We would have to take a later train. Traveling had taken its toll on our appearance, so we endeavored to use some of our time to rectify this. The train into Switzerland was also crowded. It seemed as if a large percentage of Italians were commuting to Switzerland that day. Aunts, uncles, cousins...bottles of wine and salami sandwiches...little old grandmothers and lots of children shared our coach.

One family must surely have been moving their entire household, goods and all! They staggered on with suitcases and parcels, and then relatives began to pass more packages in through the windows. The aisle became blocked as more and more belongings flowed in. Were we the only non-Italians in the coach? It surely *sounded* like it. We stood up and noticed a young man a few seats behind us reading *Time* magazine. Perhaps there were three of us, after all.

The scenery as we climbed high into the Italian Alps, then up through the pass and over into Switzerland, was breathtaking. We stopped at a little station, and many got out just to stretch their legs or buy refreshments. We opened the window and leaned out. The young man who had been reading *Time* was on the platform. When he heard Evey and me speaking English, he came over, and we invited him to sit with us. He told us he was a physicist and that he had been attending an international seminar at Lake Como. Before returning to the United States, he was going to visit friends in Geneva.

When he had finished telling us this, he asked where we had come from and where we were going. We said we had come from Albania. He showed immediate interest—he was well-informed and asked many searching questions. We needed to explain that we had entered with a tour group but that we had come out alone.

"How were you able to do this?" he asked.

As simply as we could, we told him of the reason for our arrest and of our subsequent deportation from the country. He became strangely quiet, and we sat in silence for a long time while the train sped on. Both of us knew that he needed to break the silence, not us. There was a question that he obviously wanted and needed to ask. Silently, we prayed.

At last, a little awkwardly, he said, "I happen to be Jewish. Would you think it rude if I asked you both a very personal question? How did you come to have faith in God?"

Evey answered him first and shared how the God of the Bible had become personal and real to her. Then I followed, sharing how as I had read the Bible, I had discovered the answers to the most basic questions any man can ask: "Who am I? How did I get here? Where am I going?"

A strange expression crossed his face as he admitted, "I guess I need to read the Bible. I've felt an urge to do so for some time. That ought to include the New Testament as well as the Old, I suppose?" We agreed with him, and he assured us he would begin when he reached home.

What tremendous timing! The train pulled into Lausanne just as our conversation ended. We bade him farewell, and he stood looking out the window as we rushed into the arms of friends who had come to meet us. The extra hours we had spent in Milan had enabled us to telephone and give them our arrival time. With our arrival two days overdue, their concern had been mounting.

"Tell us all about it!" they chorused. "How come you came into

Lausanne instead of Paris? How long have you been on the road—you look like tramps!"

Perhaps we looked like tramps, but we felt like millionaires—rich with the treasures of peace and joy that this world can never give nor can it take away.

Chapter Fifteen

Strive Together in Your Prayers to God for Me

Someone has said that the power of prayer cannot be diminished by distance, and it is not limited by age, infirmity, political changes, or restrictions. The power of prayer in the life of the Christian can only be undermined by neglect!

We knew before beginning our trip to Albania that prayer would be our lifeline with heaven; that as we prayed and as those with whom we had taken time to share our plans and needs prayed, the necessary spiritual supplies would be made available to us. There is no explanation for what took place during those seven days other than the fact that God's saints were found in the place of prayer. Because of prevailing intercession, God's power was released and the will of God was realized in ways that only eternity will fully reveal.

Just days after returning to Lausanne, the first of many letters began to arrive. One came from the wife of a prominent evangelist in my homeland of New Zealand. She wrote, "In my prayers it seemed as though you were to make vital contact with a woman—preplanned by God; one who would eventually be used for future work."

From a friend in America:

> I have just heard from Sylvia some of your story and I look forward to hearing more. I have to confess I was not so faithful in prayer as I should have been, though you did come to mind forcefully from time to time. I was very aware of the need for those direct lines of communication from the Lord in the difficult moments and also that there was to be some contact with a local believer, but that is all. From what Syl said, much of it was as the Lord had already revealed—including the real danger.

A friend of Evey's in England wrote:

> I had no doubts, all the way through, about your safe return nor about the Lord upholding you in whatever way you needed. I think during my times of prayer for you, I knew that you would not go through your trip without unpleasantness; and on the seventh day, I felt a greater urgency in prayer for you. On that same morning, my husband asked me if I was praying daily for you. He, too, had felt the need to uplift you on the seventh day.

Praise God for those who have gone beyond merely praying "God-bless-Mary" type of prayers, who take the time to prepare their hearts before God, and who wait and listen as God reveals the specific details that have to be prayed through.

I had recognized the need to tell my mother my summer plans, yet I did not want to alarm her unduly. In a letter some weeks before our departure, I shared that I would be taking a ten-day tour to Albania with a British friend. I added that Albania was wedged in between Greece and Yugoslavia. So little is known about this land that my news created no anxiety in her heart. Immediately after returning, however, I wrote her a full account of what had taken place. Back came a beautiful reply: "Regarding your latest news *re* Albania. I admire your zeal and rejoice that you were safely delivered. I always know there is to be an element of danger; and I just have to say if that's what you enjoy doing and feel it is necessary to continue to do, then I can only pray for your safety and leave it there."

Another member of my immediate family wrote in a slightly different vein:

> I was rather horrified to read your last letter to Mum. It is indeed nice to know that I still have you to write to. I am sure that this is what has prompted me to write now, and I know that you will accept my comments in the spirit in which they are written.
>
> I know that the Good Book says to go out into the world and teach all men, but I'm darned if I ever read that an intelligent Christian teacher should openly flout the laws of a country to do this. Surely example plays a very large part in Christian teaching; and entering a country concealing Christian literature, and then distributing it—all against the laws of that country—could hardly be classed as a good example to people today who already tend to rebel against any form of authority—parental upwards. Before you put me in my place, I'll admit that the finite will never understand and should never question the infinite. However, I write in this vein because of a natural love and concern which we have for our families. You know, I thought you were returning to Switzerland to teach, arrange courses, and fulfill secretarial duties for your organization—not try to outdo the apostle Paul on crusades into hostile lands. Nonetheless, I admire you for the work you are doing for mankind and for God, but please don't overdo it. The world needs people with your faith and your ability (End of lecture!!!)

The members of Evey's Baptist Church in England were aware of our journey and were praying, also. Her pastor, the Reverend John Caiger, wrote:

> We praise God for His gracious protection of you both. We had prayed that He would be your defense and your shield in the face of all the subtle power of the enemy.
>
> How important it is to determine the mind of God in every situation, particularly with regard to smuggling literature into a country in contravention of their rules or laws. Such a course must never be pursued lightly or carelessly—only after a clear conviction that it is the will of God. We

> must never provoke trouble for ourselves by irresponsible disregard of other people's laws. But the apostles were forbidden to teach and preach in Jerusalem, and they went straight out and continued doing so; and our own William Tyndale was burnt at the stake for smuggling Bibles into England.*

Both of these two letters touch upon a very important question. Is it ethical for the Christian to violate the laws of a government—in particular, to smuggle forbidden articles?

As a point of interest, "The Baptist" ** printed an article entitled "Bible Distribution in Eastern Europe." It stated that, according to the United Bible Society, sending Bibles by mail and having visitors bring them in openly is legal in all countries except Albania. In many parts of the world, the morality of most ministry to Communist lands is being debated by Christians. The question is not a new one; it is as old as the church, as the Reverend Caiger pointed out in his letter.

Living in Switzerland, one is forcibly reminded of the Anabaptists in the sixteenth century in this regard. They proclaimed a major separation between the kingdom of Christ and the world. Though they respected the right of magistrates to legislate and enforce laws to a certain extent, they regarded the government as an institution of the kingdom of this world and, therefore, it was not ultimately binding upon the Christian. For the Anabaptists, there was only one Master: the Lord Jesus Christ. No civil authority could usurp His Lordship in the life of the Christian disciple.

All Christians are familiar with the words of the Great Commission: "Go ye into *all* the world and preach the gospel to *every* creature." The choice is relatively simple. Whom do we obey: God or earthly governments? The United Nations Declaration of Human Rights (Article 18) states: "Everyone has the right to freedom of thought, conscience and religion: this right includes freedom to change his religion or belief, and freedom either alone or in community with others and in public or private, to manifest his belief in teaching, practice, worship, and observance."

---

* Tyndale brought in the Bibles in bales of wool and cloth, in barrels, and in sacks of flour. By the time he was arrested in 1536, they had been distributed throughout the country. His dying words were, "Lord, open the King of England's eyes!"

** *The Baptist*, Vol. 91, No. 5; published monthly in New Zealand.

When this basic right is violated in nation after nation, do we care? Do we limit our involvement to remaining in a safe place and praying for them? Is God honored when we disregard almost two-thirds of the world's peoples, even though we know they are denied the opportunity to own or read the Bible and to gather together to worship God? Even when we know many are in need of finances, clothing, food, and medicines? The question remains, "How should a Christian act when evil is in power?" Perhaps the verse that speaks most powerfully to me and dismisses from my mind and heart any confusion with regard to the above question is found in 1 Peter 2:17: "Honour all men. Love the brotherhood. Fear God. Honour the king" (KJV). I believe the whole duty of man is summed up in this verse. So far as obedience to civil law does not involve disobedience to God, we are to submit to human authorities for the Lord's sake.

An interesting letter was sent to the Swiss address we had given to the French tourist agency when registering for the journey to Albania. It was typed on plain stationery and bore no name. It was dated the ninth of July reads as follows:

> Madam:
>
> I am a traveler returning from Albania who was in the same group as Miss Reona and Evelyn (I don't know their surnames). I prefer to remain anonymous and hope that you will excuse that. We have been able to obtain your address in order to share some anxieties that we had about them. It was revealed to us that they had spread prayer books in Albania and that they were being expelled. Have they returned since? The Parisian travel agent was unable to tell us, but we thought that if their religious organization sent news of them with a word of excuse, we would probably know if this affair is really finished. [This last sentence is hard to understand, but it is an accurate translation from the French.]
>
> Please intervene in this, and with my thanks accept my best wishes.

Because the letter was written in French, it was possible to determine that the writer was a woman. We replied to her that we were indeed safely back in Switzerland, but there was no further correspondence with her.

Just one week after arriving home, a letter was delivered that we had not been expecting. It bore a French postmark and it was written by the young Parisian student who had been a member of our tour group in Albania. She was the one who had shared Mary's room and gone with us into Durres and listened as I explained to Mary why we had been arrested—the one for whom we had left the small gift of money just before being escorted to the border. Hélène wrote:

> Thank you for the money you left in my room. I wanted to say good-bye to you, but I did not because I was too much compromised. What happened to you after they told us you were expelled? I hope you had not too much trouble. Did you give those religious books to people in the street? I think it was very brave to do so, and I felt sorry for you when they interrogated you. Why did you feel you had to do it? Are you members of an organization. Maybe I am too curious, but I would like to know because I cannot blame you, though I have not the same ideas as you. I hope to hear from you very soon. Thanks ever so much for your parting present.

Hélène gave us an address to reply to in England. Immediately after returning from Albania, she had left to take part in a Shakespearean course at Cambridge University. Gladly, both of us replied to her most important question, "Why did you feel you had to do it?"

Hélène's second letter was dated the twenty-first of August:

> Thank you very much for your letters. I was very pleased to hear from you. When I was in England, I went to visit Mary for a weekend, and it was good to see her again. I enjoyed my stay in Cambridge—I learned a lot of things about Shakespeare (I read ten plays in English) and about modern literature as well.
>
> If you don't mind, I'd like to ask you further questions about religion. How can you be sure that God exists? There is no material proof, and how can you know that what is written in the Bible is truth? Besides, there are so many various religions in the world that they seem to be relative, not

> universal. You would have another religion if you were born in Asia, for instance. Atheism rejects religion because people who believe in God rely on Him and struggle for a better world to live in on earth. Atheism is based upon man and upon his power to transform Nature. Man relies on his own strength; nobody else helps him. If all men were struggling for solidarity, peace, and friendship on earth, they would achieve something great and transform Nature by themselves. My last question is, Why does God let people suffer and die and kill one another at war if He exists and loves them? I'm very happy to be able to discuss about all these things with you, and I'm very grateful to you for taking trouble to answer me.

Again we replied individually, addressing ourselves to her three major questions. In addition, we enclosed with our letters some booklets by Floyd McClung, plus a tape by Loren Cunningham entitled, "Why Do the Innocent Suffer?"

Her reply came, dated the twenty-seventh of September:

> Thank you for the two booklets you sent me. I have skimmed through them, but I'm going to read them carefully in the next few days. For the moment I find myself in a very uncomfortable position as I can't deny my left-wing political ideas, and yet I am puzzled at the same time by the question of life and the beginning of the world. I don't know what to think. It would have been better for me not to study philosophy at school.
>
> I am ashamed of my behavior when I think of good, militant Communists, and yet I think I must try to get an answer to the questions that are puzzling me. If I am with other left-wing students during the year, I think I'll forget these questions for a while. It's very difficult to live in this world. Anyway, you can't imagine how much comfort it is for me to keep in touch with you. I love you very much as my eldest sisters.
>
> With much love, Hélène.

Shortly after this, I left Europe to spend some time in the United States and New Zealand, while Evey remained in Lausanne, continuing her work as a midwife. As I traveled and shared the Albanian experience, I told of the young Marxist-Leninist who was asking such searching questions about God and Christianity. As a result, many began to pray that her search might end like Paul's—in a personal confrontation with the Lord Jesus Christ.

Correspondence with her continued to flow. In late November she wrote:

> I have just returned from the Congress of France—USSR, which took place at Royan, a seaside resort in the southwest of France. We were about 400 delegates from all over the country. It gave me the opportunity to discuss with many people, and I think it's very important for peace in the world to try to understand other people's opinions.
>
> I'd love to hear from you soon. Remember, a letter from you comforts me and helps me find the right way.
>
> Much love from your little sister, Hélène.

She was searching for the answers to many questions, and we invited her to come to Lausanne as soon as possible and stay for a few days. She came on the thirty-first of December, able to spend only two days. She stayed with Evey, as I was still in New Zealand. Her first evening, Evey asked her if she would like to come to the school. The new students had just arrived, all 70 of them, from many different nations, and would be introducing themselves and sharing a little about their lives. Hélène agreed to come. She sat very quietly and made few comments after it, but Evey could see that she was thinking deeply. The next day, after they relaxed together, Hélène stated she would like to go back to the school for her second evening. On this occasion, the students were answering the fourth Quaker question: "When did God become more than a word to you?" (The Quaker questions are four questions designed to introduce members of a group quickly to one another.) Hélène listened as each student gave a personal testimony to the saving life of Christ. The next day she returned to Paris.

Within a week, Evey received a letter from her.

> I had a good journey home and arrived in Paris at eight. Thank you so much for my wonderful stay in Lausanne. These two days really were the happiest of my

life. I didn't know that there were so many real Christians and that love could change people in such a way. Now I am sure that God exists and that He loves me. I can't tell you in words how happy I am to have found it out and how grateful I am to you who have helped me so much since we first met in Albania. Of course, I still have a lot to learn about the Lord—about prayer and how to serve Him.

On Friday, I really felt the need to read the Bible. I began to read the Gospel of John, and I had a look at other parts, but I find the Old Testament hard to understand as there are so many names of people and places I have never heard of. The Gospel of John attracts me because it makes me feel the love of the Lord, but what I find hard to believe are the miracles made by Jesus. So I have still to search and think about it.

Do you know that a new idea came into my mind? I think that it isn't useless for me to have been a Communist before because I can understand people who are Communists, and maybe I could help them to find the Truth when I go to Eastern European countries. I can help the Christians who live there, too. What I want to do later is to be an interpreter because I feel it is wonderful to try to make people understand one another and so respect and love one another.

Maybe all I've said is a bit confused, but such things and feelings are so hard to express in words. Hoping to hear from you soon.

Love from your little sister.

To me she wrote:

You know, it really was in Albania that my search for truth began, when I thought about what you had been doing there. My first reaction was anger and amazement, but when I think of it now, it seems as if all had been carefully planned. This journey was for me to relax after my exam at the Science Po, as I was waiting for the results. Since then, I have been searching for six months, and now I've found the Truth. I've found true peace and joy through Jesus Christ. I have never been so happy in my life! Oh, what can I do but praise the Lord for His great love for us!

> My life has really been changed utterly, and some friends of mine are amazed at the change. I feel the need of a personal relationship with God. I feel the need to read the Bible, and I feel it is much more than going to church simply as a habit. It's rather difficult to express, but I think that after such an experience of prayer and love in Lausanne, I just must praise and thank the Lord for all that He has already done for me and for all that He has in store for me in the future. I am finding so many opportunities to praise Him, even at rush hours in the ugly Paris underground!
>
> Oh, but do write to me soon. I know that a letter is a poor substitute to a heart-to-heart conversation, but I know that you can understand feelings that words cannot express. I'm so poor in love in front of the love that Jesus has for us.
>
> Much love from your little sister.

Hélène's name had been written in the eternal records of heaven, and we had gained a very precious little sister. We communicated by letter until her next visit to Lausanne, which was in March. Already she had found a church in Paris in which to become active and had witnessed to her newfound faith in the waters of baptism. The reality of her new life was plainly evident.

A letter in February read:

> The love of Jesus for us is really amazing and wonderful. It's great to share this joy, peace and love with other Christians. I'm discovering so many wonderful things in the Bible—it really is amazing! There is an answer to each one of our needs. Every day I'm discovering wonderful things the Lord has been doing for us. God has been so good to make me aware of His love and to convince me that He is the Truth. I just sought deeply and honestly, and the Lord revealed Himself to me and showed me I had to be humble and obedient.
>
> At first my parents didn't understand my change at all. But now they seem to be less angry about it. I just trust the Lord and pray for them. I hope they will find the joy and peace and love of God one day. It's just wonderful to think of all my dear brothers and sisters in God's family. Even if

we are separated by a long distance, we are never lonely. We are all united.

I marvel at all I've been learning since the beginning of this year. I'll never be thankful enough for all that Jesus did for me. I can only praise Him with all my heart. Could you pray that the Lord makes me more obedient to Him and that He gives me more strength so that I can bring other people to Jesus?

Your little sister.

Hélène's time with us in March was very blessed as the Holy Spirit brought a new dimension into her Christian experience. We spoke together at this time about the summer, of how Lausanne had been chosen as the host city for the World Congress on Evangelization, and of how workers were needed to staff this conference—particularly those who spoke several languages. Lausanne had also been chosen as the place for Evey's summer wedding. Hélène did not need more persuasion to come. And so, the one who as a committed Marxist had worked toward the goal of the takeover of the entire earth for the cause of communism now worked under the banner of the Congress, which had taken as its motto, "Let the Earth Hear His Voice!" What a reversal, and in such a short space of time!

Continuing her university studies in Paris, in the early summer of 1975 Hélène graduated with a degree in economics from the Science Po and a degree in Russian from the Sorbonne. What was she to do now? Why had she felt led to study Polish for the last two years? In late July, a month after her graduation, we found ourselves together in Poland as two members of a team of four, invited to speak and teach at student youth camps in the south of the country.

In a barn that served as a chapel, I heard her give her testimony. With every sentence, her identification with Polish young people became more evident. She, too, had been born into a predominantly Roman Catholic nation and had been at Roman Catholic schools. But in her early teens, she searched for the reality of the theory that was always being given to her. That word *love* was used so often, but why was there so little evidence of it at work? It was then that she began seriously to study other philosophies. Marxism seemed to come closest to what she was looking for. She understood the need to give herself totally to these principles. The only thing that really bothered her was that, to achieve their goals, Marxists were prepared to use violence, if there was no other way to bring about the required revolution. Yet such was her commitment when in Russia that she was impressed with almost everything she saw. But then came the tour of Albania!

Hélène had never met or known Christians who were as committed to Christ as Marxists were to their cause. Her curiosity was aroused. As she asked her questions and received answers, a flame was kindled in her heart. Then she came to Lausanne. After her first evening at the school, she went home and prayed her first prayer in many years: "God, if You exist, reveal Yourself to me." When she woke up in the morning, she knew there was a God and that He cared for her and was able to give her the life she had searched so hard to find. The same dedication that had been given to the Communist cause was now applied to the Christian life. The basis of her message to the Polish young people was 1 John 4:9-10: "In this was manifested the love of God toward us, because that God sent his only begotten Son into the world, that we might live through him. Herein is love, not that we loved God, but that he loved us, and sent his Son to be the propitiation for our sins" (KJV).

True to her word given the week of her conversion, she was now in Eastern Europe.

Understanding the Communist philosophy, she pointed young Communists to the truth which had so revolutionized her life, and at the same time she spoke from her heart to the Christians in that land. She convinced them that the gospel is still the power of God unto salvation to everyone who believes—and that the heart of the most dedicated, radical Marxist can be melted by the pursuing love of a God who cares and is able to forgive and redeem.

CHAPTER SIXTEEN

Every Knee Shall Bow and Every Tongue Confess

Lord, what wilt Thou have me to do?

As God's servants have begun to bring the needs of the nation of Albania before the body of Christ, and as Christians have begun (where all work for God must begin) to intercede before the throne for this land and its people, significant changes are occurring. In 1973, the pope rightly referred to Albania as "the church of silence"—a land where no churches were open or functioning, where no Christians were in touch with the outside world. But that is no longer so. Major newspapers in Europe, and magazines such as *Time* and *Newsweek* are beginning to glean information and print it; the number of tour groups entering each summer is increasing, and Albania is establishing diplomatic relations with additional countries. Is this the natural consequence of events, or is this a result of persevering prayer—the sort of prayer that lays hold of God and reminds Him that for these people His Son died?

In December of 1973, an article written by Richard Wurmbrand entitled, "Evangelical Action for the Silent Church" was printed in a French publication. He detailed some of the suffering endured for Christ's sake in that land:

The Bishop of Durres, in Communist Albania, was enclosed in an iron cage the size of his body. The inside walls were covered with iron spikes which entered into his flesh. The cage was pushed along the streets until he died.

Franco Gjiri, priest from Mirdizia, was enclosed for 68 days in a stone cell one meter square. Pieces of wood were forced under his nails. He was given electric shocks and then he was beaten. Yet, he arrived for his execution encouraging his brethren.

To brother Peter Koskava, the Communists said, "Talk against God and you will be saved." To which he replied, "I have given my life to Christ; I cannot speak against Him, but only against you, the oppressors."

The old, old priest Slako was beaten in full view of all the street until he died, for having said the rosary aloud.

The last words of a priest named Macai before being beaten were "Long live Christ our King!"

Early in 1974, a major Swedish newspaper printed an article, "Intensified Persecution Against Christians in Albania." It reads as follows:

> The first atheistic state in the world, Albania, is having difficulties with signs of religious life within the country. This is in spite of intense persecution by the authorities against all Christian and other religious activity during the last decade. In Durres, the largest port city in the country, the secret police have discovered underground Christian activity as well as pilgrimages. Pictures of saints, which were supposed to have been destroyed, are kept in secret and are being used. In spite of the risk of losing their lives, priests visit homes in civil clothing and perform baptism and wedding ceremonies in ordinary church fashion. In a circular distributed within the central committee of the Communist party, the strategy for the battle against religion in the near future was presented. The Party leaders are determined to enforce atheism BY ANY MEANS that will be necessary. Those who refuse to participate in atheistic seminars will be subject to police actions.

In the summer of 1974, two significant events took place. A Slavic worker was arrested in Yugoslavia for giving out Christian literature and was imprisoned. He discovered, once in prison, that the majority of his fellow prisoners were Albanians. (More than one million Albanians live in Yugoslavia.) Grateful for unlimited time to share with them the gospel of Christ, he saw not one or two, but a much larger number confess Jesus Christ as Lord.

Large Albanian communities are also located on the East Coast of the United States, particularly in the Boston area, and in southeastern Australia. At the very time we were preparing to enter the land in 1973, we received a letter from a young Albanian/Australian who had been recently converted and was already recognizing a call to return to the land of his birth, in God's time and way.

There are more than two million gypsies in Europe (in Spain and France, in Italy and Romania, in Poland and Yugoslavia), and God is at work in their hearts and has used them to evangelize Albania.

In the early summer of 1974, a group of gypsies had gathered for a feast close to the Albanian border. One night, as they looked at the towering mountains that separated them from the land of Albania, they asked among themselves, "What is there to stop us from going over the mountains?" They agreed there was nothing to prevent their doing this. Several members of the group had relatives in Albania and had crossed into the country quite often—illegally, of course. One man had been sent a large amount of Christian literature in the Albanian language. So over the mountains they went and entered into what had been predominantly Moslem villages. With great boldness, they spoke to the people about Jesus and gave out their literature. The response was surprising. The people were eager to read, and they asked question after question about the Christian faith. After continuing in this manner for 11 days, they were arrested and held in the local police station for two weeks. They continued their work while in prison and were secretly released to return over the mountains, the same way they had come.

"*...if by any means I might preach the gospel*"!

Two other means of evangelizing Albania are also being employed. Weekly, Trans World Radio beams in programs from its station in Monte Carlo, and another mission encloses Scripture portions and other Christian literature in bottles and releases them in Italy to float across the Adriatic.

And what of the political atmosphere in the land? It, too, is changing. An article entitled "Albania—Plus Ça Change" appeared in *Newsweek*, November 11, 1974. Part of the article reads as follows:

> Enver Hoxha, who has been Albania's comrade-in-chief for 30 years, has never been one to mince his words about the threats he sees across his tiny country's borders. "Forces of darkness," he stormed, in a typical speech earlier this year, "advise us to open the door for swine, for people with hot pants and even without pants, for hippies who would replace our beautiful folk dances with wild orgies. They are trying to corrupt our country, organize putsches, and set up military bases." Thus, it came as a shock last month when the hard-hitting Hoxha delivered a speech that seemed to suggest a waning of Albania's paranoid xenophobia. In an election address, Comrade Hoxha had unusually warm words for Greece and Yugoslavia and even declared that "in France, Scandinavia, and Belgium, we have many friends."
>
> This is a significant statement in view of the fact that Hoxha has been so concerned lest any outside influence corrupt his nation. He has even gone so far as to block the reception of television from foreign sources which was obtainable in the mountain areas.
>
> Since Albania is still among the most primitive countries in Europe, it seemed logical if uncharacteristic for Hoxha to seek rapprochement with the West. But it now appears that Hoxha's real message was little changed. As China's only ally among the Communist leaders west of Suez, Hoxha was apparently outraged by recent suggestions from his Defense Minister, Bequir Balluku, that Albania ought to soften its hard line against the Soviet Union. In short, Hoxha's references to "friends" in the West were intended to assure Albanians that his foreign policy, far from needing a change, was already quite open enough.
>
> Proof of all this came last week when the 66-year-old Hoxha announced a new government. In so doing, he unceremoniously dumped his Defense Minister and the ruling Politburo. The errant Balluku, it appeared, had suddenly become a nonperson—no mean feat in a country of only two million people.

More recently still, *Time*, August 18, 1975, commenting on the Security Conference in Helsinki which had just ended, included this comment: "Yugoslavia has improved its traditionally hostile relations with neighboring Albania, Peking's surrogate in Europe and the only State that boycotted the Soviet's cherished Security Conference in Helsinki."

The prayers of God's people are effecting change in the land. However, the words of Isaiah 42:22-23 remain terribly true:

> But this is a people plundered and looted,
> all of them trapped in pits or hidden away in prisons.
> They have become plunder, with no one to rescue them;
> they have been made loot, with no one to say, "Send them back."
> Which of you will listen to this
> or pay close attention in time to come?

But the struggle continues. On March 24, 1976, a Christian daily newspaper in Holland called *Trouw* printed the following statement, entitled "Albania Removes the Church from the Constitution." The dateline is Tirana.

> Albania has adapted its Constitution to the attitude it has held for many years regarding religion and the church. In the new Constitution which will be announced shortly, Albania will be officially declared an atheistic State, and all forms of religion will be made illegal.
>
> According to the old Constitution, all citizens, regardless of their race or religion, were equal. That has now been finished with, and each parent must bring up his children without religion. Personal rights are subjected to the general interest.
>
> Party leader Enver Hoxha said a short while ago that religion did not disappear when the church buildings and mosques did. "The battle against habits, traditions, and religious institutions which have deep roots in our people, has not yet come to an end. It is a tough, long, complicated battle," said Hoxha, who also pointed to the fact that young people remain insensitive to religion.

Shortly before his death, Chairman Mao described Chinese-Albanian friendship as "inexhaustible and truly invincible." In the period following Mao's death, however, relations between China and its Balkan prodigy steadily deteriorated. The origins of the quarrel lay in Albania's hostility to China's policy of rapprochement with the United States and the Third World and to Peking's warming relations with Albania's longtime enemy, Yugoslavia. Instead of trying to patch up the quarrel, Peking apparently decided it was time to end the drain on China's resources—more than four billion dollars since 1954! (China claimed to have given aid to Albania in quantities second only to its aid to Vietnam.)

On July 7, 1978, 513 Chinese military advisors and technicians departed from Albania, leaving behind 51 uncompleted aid projects. According to the official Chinese news agency, Peking had been showering grain, steel, tractors, and trucks on the ungrateful Albanians when China could not spare them. Help had been given, the Chinese claimed, with 142 projects, 91 of which had been completed. In addition, China had sent 6,000 technicians to work in Albania, and 2,000 Albanians were trained in China. The Chinese people scrimped on food and clothing and tried their best to aid Albania in the spirit of proletarian internationalism, the news agency complained. Albania is accused of base ingratitude, slander, and sabotage in return for fraternal solidarity. In reply, the Albanians accused China of impairing its European ally's defense by disclosing military secrets and performing a perfidious and hostile act in scrapping economic and military aid. A 16,000-word letter circulated in Tirana, Albania's capital. It was addressed to the Central Committee and the State Council of China: "With this hostile step against socialist Albania," the letter charged, "you seek to hit and damage the economy and defense of our country, to sabotage the cause of the revolution and socialism in Albania."

It was a repetition, the letter stated, of the savage and chauvinistic methods of Tito and Khruschev and Brezhnev. In retaliation, Tirana radio has stopped relaying 145 hours a week of Chinese propaganda broadcasts in English, French, Spanish, Portuguese, Italian, Czech, Serbo-Croation, Turkish, and Hausa.

Moscow radio, seeking perhaps to woo Albania, called the Chinese action an act of "unprincipled perfidy," adding that the Albanians now obviously realize that their former attitude toward the Soviet Union and its allies was erroneous.

We believe that all earthly powers are subject to our Almighty God and that Albania will have to capitulate when those called by

God to enter the land, in faith set their feet upon its soil. Prayer is clearing the way for God's pioneers to go in. Earlier in this century, when it was still possible—though dangerous—to enter China as a missionary, a young woman prepared to go there. A friend asked of her, "Are you not afraid?" She replied, "I am afraid of only one thing—that I will become a grain of wheat unwilling to die."

Many times Evey and I have sought God to know the reasons why we were released from Albania. We believe that in these days God wants to assure His people that He is as great as His Word declares Him to be—the strong and Mighty One, able to save and deliver all those who put their trust in Him. But more than this, He seeks to prepare His people, to draw them so close to His heart that they will not love their lives even unto death, but will offer themselves to the great Sower of seed, as grains of wheat willing to die.

The King is returning, and before Him every knee shall bow and every tongue shall confess that Jesus Christ is Lord, to the glory of God the Father.

To us has been entrusted the privilege of hastening the day of His return by causing the ancient gates to yield and the Bamboo and Iron curtains to crumble before the manifest life of the risen Lord Jesus.

Hélène Anger Update

When I read again the story told in this book, I am overwhelmed to see the goodness, the patience, and the love which the Lord has bestowed on me, and I can only thank Him for His faithfulness and forgiveness. He pursued me with His love even to Albania—a country which openly claimed to be the first atheistic state in the world. Nothing is impossible with God—no government, no man-made border can separate us from His love.

I also would like to thank all those who interceded for me perseveringly and especially Reona and Evey. Their commitment to serve and follow God was for me a mighty and unquestionable testimony—an example as well as a challenge. The desire was awakened in me to know more about Him who gave meaning to their lives and would lead them according to His ways.

I received teaching on the character and ways of God in attending the Discipleship Training School run by Youth With A Mission in Denmark in 1976-1977. The Lord has done a deepening work in my spirit and in my thoughts. He made the scales fall from my eyes which had blinded me to His vision of the world. Ever since then, I have had the opportunity to put my knowledge of the Russian language at His disposal in reaching out to others and also in going into Eastern Europe. During journeys to these countries, I could see the faithfulness and protection of God. He is at work to strengthen and enlarge His church. Surely, the needs are great and vary much from one country to the other, but God can meet them, and He wants to quench the thirst for truth that characterizes the younger generation.

The plans of the Lord are perfect. He can utilize and transform all these things for His glory as He is doing it in the smallest details of my life to prepare me to serve Him in Eastern Europe. Intercession is the most effective weapon available to us to reach that target, and it is the solid basis upon which it is possible to build

God's kingdom. Thus, we have the privilege of taking part in the advancement of His kingdom in this world. The Lord is faithful and His Spirit comes to our aid in our weakness.

The time is short. Strengthened by His help, are we going to wholly accept the responsibility He has entrusted to us? This book shows the power of God in response to prayer and the obedience of His servants, and it gives me a personal challenge—that of committing myself more to intercession and to seeing the will of the Lord accomplished in various countries of the world, even the most impossible.

Hélène Anger
January 1979

Epilogue

Albania, indeed one of the most "impossible" of countries, has undergone radical change. How can this change be explained? I believe above every other explanation is this simple but profound response: God has heard and answered the intercession of multitudes of people who have prayed for this land.

With amazing speed, Albania has thrown off the shackles of nearly 50 years of brutal Communist rule. Enver Hoxha died in 1985. An ever-worsening economic crisis pushed his successor, Ramiz Ala, into introducing mild reforms. But it was the overthrow of the Ceausescu regime in Romania in 1989 that served as a catalyst for Albanian youth to begin their own relatively bloodless revolution. It was only a matter of time before the last Communist "domino" in Eastern Europe would fall.

Slowly at first, Albania began to open its doors to the outside world. In the summer of 1991, permission was given to rent one of Tirana's football stadiums for a week of Christian meetings.

In March 1992, free and democratic elections were held, and a 48-year-old cardiologist, Sali Berisha, was elected president. He promised his people democracy, the return of human rights, freedom of speech, and hope for the future. We can only continue to pray to that end.

Since 1991, Youth With A Mission workers from many nations have joined the ever-increasing army of Christians determined to follow in the footsteps of the apostle Paul and fully preach the gospel of Christ in Illyricum (Romans 15:19). It is now believed that there are more missionaries per capita in Albania—some 300 for three million people—than anywhere else in the world!

What have they been able to accomplish?

A fellow-missionary organization has summarized it in this manner:

"The gospel of Jesus Christ is again being heard throughout this long forgotten land. What is happening can be compared to the creation story of Genesis. The following is the King James version with minor changes to explain God's plan and new creation in Albania.

"In the beginning, God created Albania and it was without form and it was void of any existence of God. The Spirit of God moved across Albania and communism had its downfall.

"And God said, 'Let there be light.' Albania had been in total spiritual darkness for 47 years. Missionaries came in 1991 bringing with them the Gospel of Light. And God saw the light, that it was good and God divided the light from the darkness as many thousands of Albanians gave their lives to Christ in the early crusades.

"And God called it a new day. 7,000 came to the Lord within 2 years. And God said, 'Let there be a commotion in the midst of the water.' Many new believers have been baptized in the waters of Albania. More than 40 churches having been established—united in their belief in God. And God said, 'Let the churches be gathered under the heavens.' 1200 people from 7 churches gathered in Tirana to celebrate a Risen Savior on Easter Day.

"And God said, 'Let the churches bring forth pastors and teachers, yielding fruits after its kind.' And God said, 'Let there be lights in the heavens for signs.' These signs are evident as former communists are changed from within, people are healed from illnesses, and families are brought together—peace reigns in the hearts of men. A diversification of skills has come to Albania, because God has sent different kinds of lights to shine upon her.

"And God said, 'Let there be creatures that move and fly.' God has opened doors in radio and television. Hundreds of thousands of people have heard and seen the gospel. A complete Bible in the Albanian language has been published. Bible courses have been translated to assist the discipling of new believers.

"Members of parliament, lawyers, doctors, common people, even former theives make up the church's congregation. Those who are in great need are helped by the people of God—food, electricity, water, new businesses.

"And God said, 'Let us make man in our image.' Albanians now stand tall in self-respect and go to the villages and preach His Word. Their very lives are examples of the life-changing power that faith in Jesus Christ produces."

Prior to Communism, Albania's history was rooted in Christianity. Now Albanians can be a reflection of the creative and life-changing power of their Creator to whom they have returned. God's people have been sent to Albania to proclaim His truths to these people. The Church is alive and growing and multiplying. His peace that passes all understanding is in the hearts of His people, for God is great and has done the impossible.

Throughout Albania's history, the nation has found it advantageous to change its religion according to who was in power, thus the proverb, "Ku ështē shpata ështē feja." Where the sword, there lies religion.

The Christian message is not unchallenged. Islam is resurgent, and the cults are strongly represented. Materialism grips the hearts of many, after being denied for so long even a basic standard of living.

The Balkan spirits of disunity, deceit, fear, generational hatred, and resentments help to feed such traditions as the "Code of Revenge." (A man was beheaded with an ax in a Tirana hotel lobby in 1992 in revenge for a killing his father had committed in a northern village more than 40 years before.) This "Code of Revenge" forms a major part of society in the remote mountainous regions.

Along with much-needed humanitarian aid, moral and spiritual renewal is of equal importance.

But I am not discouraged—quite the reverse. Imprisoned in 1973 for daring to bring a small quantity of Christian literature into the land, for the past five years I have returned annually for the express purpose of sharing my faith and teaching new Christians principles of discipleship based on God's Word. In 1992, within 30 minutes of driving into Durres, I had found Stefani. Durres, the major port city in Albania with a population in excess of 80,000 and a string of tourist hotels along its fine beaches, was where I was held in 1973. Stefani worked in the hotel and had revealed to me that she was a Christian.

Subsequent visits in 1993 and 1994 answered the lingering questions that had remained with me for nineteen years. Stefani had not betrayed me by handing the booklet I gave her to the authorities. In fact, she still had it in her possession. Evey, my companion, had been discovered leaving a booklet on a park bench in the south of the country, that prompted first my arrest and then hers. Stefani, a wife, mother, and grandmother, is the daughter of an Orthodox priest, and she and her family have remained true to the Christian faith throughout the Communist era.

A further stanza from Byron's *Childe Harold* seems appropriate:

Land of Albania! Let me bend mine eye on thee, thou rugged nurse of savage men! The cross descends, thy minarets arise, and the pale crescent sparkles in the glen through many a cypress grove with each city's ken.

The contest between the cross and the minaret continues. Please take time to thank God for the unyoking of Eastern Europe in recent years and please, as you do, pause and pray specifically for Albania and its three million people. Pray that in this nation where the very existence of God was so vehemently denied, the knowledge of the glory of the Lord will cover the land even as the waters cover the sea.

"Zoti Ju Bekofte Shume!" May you be truly blessed!

Reona Peterson Joly